He Was

What other man could have faced down that whole terrace of strangers as if they didn't matter?

Then he surprised her. As he came to the last step—their faces were almost level, but he still had to lower his eyes to look into hers—he smiled at her. He really was different, more intense or something. He was conscious of her. Why hadn't he shown this much interest in her at her apartment? Her nerves were in a state, and she couldn't do anything except stare back.

A tingling swept through her body. Astonishing. All those men there in that place had had no effect on her at all, but when Quint showed up, she became weak-kneed and pliant.

Why was she so attracted to this man?

Because he was like no other.

Dear Reader:

I hope you've been enjoying 1989, our "Year of the Man" at Silhouette Desire. Every one of the twelve authors who are contributing a *Man of the Month* has created a very special someone for your reading pleasure. Each man is unique, and each author's style, plot and characterization give you a different insight into her man's story.

From January to December, 1989 will be a twelve-month extravaganza, spotlighting one book each month with special cover treatment as a tribute to the Silhouette Desire hero—our *Man of the Month*!

You'll find these men who've been created by your favorite authors irresistible. Naomi Horton's Slater McCall is indeed *A Dangerous Kind of Man*, coming this April, and love, betrayal, greed and revenge are all part of Lucy Gordon's dramatic *Vengeance Is Mine*, featuring Luke Harmon as Mr. May.

Don't let these men get away!

Yours,

Isabel Swift
Senior Editor & Editorial Coordinator

LASS SMALL
Red Rover

Silhouette Desire

Published by Silhouette Books New York
America's Publisher of Contemporary Romance

SILHOUETTE BOOKS
300 East 42nd St., New York, N.Y. 10017

ISBN: 0-373-05491-2

First Silhouette Books printing April 1989

Printed in the U.S.A.

Books by Lass Small

Silhouette Romance

An Irritating Man #444
Snow Bird #521

Silhouette Desire

Tangled Web #241
To Meet Again #322
Stolen Day #341
Possibles #356
Intrusive Man #373
To Love Again #397
Blindman's Bluff #413
Goldilocks and the Behr #437
Hide and Seek #453
Red Rover #491

LASS SMALL

finds that living on this planet at this time is a fascinating experience. People are amazing. She thinks that to be a teller of tales about people, places and things is absolutely marvelous.

One

___

It was just before Christmas, and only about three weeks after he'd met Georgina Lambert in Texas, that Quintus Finnig turned up at her place in Sacramento, California. Irritated that he would be there, he walked into her building after barely flashing a meaningless wallet picture at the bored man by the door.

Quint found her apartment on the second floor, halfway down the hall and on the left. He leaned against the panel next to her door as he checked his watch. He didn't have long to wait before Georgina came down the carpeted hall toward him, still shaking droplets from her raincoat.

When George saw Quint standing at her door, waiting for her, she didn't break stride. All her theatrical training came to her rescue. Only superb control allowed her to continue walking toward him. She was really impressed that she didn't fall against the wall, unable to move because her knees were so weakened when she saw him. She even managed to smile as she said "Well, hello."

Quint was disgruntled that she showed no surprise—at all—that he was there. Being the blunt man that he was, he replied to her greeting with, "Security in this building's lousy. Anybody could walk in here, Georgina." In his own mind, those were the concerned words of a lover.

George was intensely aware that while everyone else called her "George," Quint had called her "Georgina" since they had first met last November in Texas.

She tilted her head just a little. She met any number of people on her travels and now and then, one turned up on her doorstep. Quint's appearance shouldn't be such a surprise, but in seeing him so unexpectedly, she found she was a little witless and she struggled to appear normal.

Seizing upon the subject of the building's security, she came very close to babbling. "Sacramento is the state capital, and it's filled with people who are in or deal with the state government. All the citizens here are honest, wholesome people who think only of the public good. Don't look so dubious. In this great state of California, the citizens are devoted to law and order, and therefore—" She sighed and opened her purse to find her key. "You don't look like you're receptive to my explanation."

Since Georgina's attention was on finding the door key, she couldn't see the hungry look he sent over her slender body. She thought he wasn't receptive? "You oughta have the key ready. If you hunt for it, just standing there, some guy could hit you over the head or push you inside and slam the door. Pay attention."

She looked at him.

He stared back.

Each felt the wash of the almost overwhelming attraction that had been between them since they first saw each other down in Texas.

With barely muffled curiosity, she inquired, "What brings you to California?"

How couldn't she know? "Personal business," he replied gruffly. That was true. He had to see if the attraction was real or imaginary. It was real. Now he had to figure out what to do about her.

Georgina waited for him to say something, and when he didn't, she recalled that he was an unusually silent man. "Have you time for a small libation?" she asked. "It's been a bear cat of a day. Come in, won't you?"

He looked at the sweetness of her, at her blond hair and blue eyes. She didn't look at all dangerous to him. But she was. She could ruin him.

He walked into her apartment expecting to hear dramatic music that matched his mood, just like in the movies. But there wasn't any. Then he thought maybe the silence was more telling.

Little shivers of excitement flickered in George's body. She'd never expected to see him again. Uninvited, he'd arrived at the double wedding last November when her eldest sister Tate married Bill Sawyer and her youngest sister Hillary married Angus Behr. In that crowd of people at her parents' house, and without any effort on his part, he'd commanded attention. George had felt hesitant about approaching him, as if in wanting to know him, she was moving into strangely thrilling but perhaps dangerous territory.

She had been almost immobilized with her body's reaction to him. She was used to men noticing her, but to her knowledge, Quint hadn't responded to her in the least. Although he'd danced with her, he had made no effort to become more than a dancing partner. Finally, by the end of their three-day acquaintance, she'd given up trying to make him acknowledge his awareness of her, as a woman, by a gesture or look.

The only time she'd caught him really looking at her was when the five Lambert sisters had come down the stairs together for the wedding. For once, George had found his gaze on her, and he hadn't turned away. Other than that, he hadn't sought her out especially. Yet every time she'd looked up, she'd known he'd be there, and he was. But after he left, she'd not heard from him at all, and she finally relinquished him.

So, why was he in Sacramento? At her apartment? In some disgust, George remembered that Tate and Bill were back in Chicago after their honeymoon. Quint had probably mentioned to them that he had business in California, so more than likely they'd asked him to check up on her. Coming to see her hadn't been his idea, after all. But still, he *was* there.

On a pass-through to the dining room, George kept a small tray to serve as a small bar. Quint took a shot glass of Scotch and sipped it occasionally while George mixed herself a wine spritzer. She took a sip, then went into the living room, with Quint following. There she sat on the sofa and kicked off her shoes. He looked at her stockinged feet in such an intense way that she thought she probably seemed vulgar to him. She figured he must not have any sisters.

Quint thought that to him, a man who'd worked in a strip joint as a kid, the sight of Georgina's stockinged feet shouldn't affect him so strongly. Why did everything about Georgina set him on his ear? He moved stiffly to the window and stood with his back to her.

In order to fill the silence, George told about her day. "We've a client who has trouble facing a camera. He's as glib as a carny barker ordinarily, but put a camera in front of him and he freezes."

Quint turned back toward her. "What's your job?"

He was much too blunt. George cocked her head and smiled at him. "I'm a media trainer. I train people to handle speaking before an audience or to an inquiring cameraperson. People who can run multibillion-dollar businesses can become mute at the sight of an audience looking toward them, or if a microphone is pushed at them. And a hostile interviewer can drive them to babbling panic. We teach them how they can handle it all."

Quint could well understand the need to learn to talk under pressure. He might forfeit his soul to be able to talk to Georgina. She had changed him. He'd been reading poetry for almost a month, ever since he'd met this woman.

George went on. "It's a rather new service. Presidents have had coaching since television came into being, but now anyone who is a politician, or a CEO or a spokesperson, or anyone who handles publicity for any business, needs to be able to handle an interviewer, hostile or not. It actually comes down to anyone in the public eye. We can help."

Yeah, he thought. Then there was Quint Finnig, who was so zonked by a woman that only God could help him. "You need to tell maintenance that tree branch oughta be cut off. It's too close to your window."

She had to take several breaths before she managed to gasp, *"Cut off that limb?* "You're crazy! That branch is all I see of the outside world in the whole, entire day. If I lost that, I would never see anything real."

"There's trees in this town."

"I drive, and I watch where I drive. I don't look at the scenery. I park in a parking garage. I take the elevator to the office, and I have an inner office. I don't rate a window yet, but I will some day. Then after five, I go to the garage, get in my car and come home to that tree limb." She pointed to the cherished branch.

He wasn't interested in tree branches. "You just come home? Don't you . . . go out with . . . anybody?"

"Now and then."

"You gotta watch out for men."

She thought he blushed, and she was amazed by his shyness.

Quint felt his blood pressure elevate. The very thought of her being kissed by another man made him hostile. No woman had ever called up such possessive feelings in him, and self-protection made him brace himself against her. He didn't need this. He'd come out here to exorcise her from his dreams, knowing she couldn't possibly be what he remembered, but he'd found that she was. He was so unsettled by her, and by his reaction to her, that he was silent.

Georgina realized that this could be her last opportunity to attract him. Wanting him to respond to her, she tried all the social ploys to get him into a conversation, but she failed. That didn't ordinarily bother her. She'd met a lot of men who were awkward with women; it was nothing new. She could help a hesitant client, but she couldn't coax Quint into talking. Perhaps he was comfortable with silence. So was she. She spent her days in the ramifications of speech, so she appreciated silence. But she longed to feel closer to Quint, and as she coped with the strange little quiverings that disturbed the secret places deep inside her, she was also frustrated with his lack of response.

She studied him quite openly—that was easy since he rarely looked at her. He wasn't gorgeous, although he certainly was marvelously made. He was probably close to forty; that would make him seven to nine years older than she. His hair was brown, and so were his eyes. If you only glanced at him, you'd think he was rather anonymous looking. But if you paid attention, you would realize that in whatever he did, he was a power.

What kind of power? There were all kinds of people in this world who wielded all kinds of influence—good and bad. Which was he? Just the fact that she was unsure of his place in the world was an indication of the kind of man he could be. In George's mind, there lurked the nagging question as to why, last November in Texas, her new brothers-in-law had tried to ease Quint Finnig out of the Lambert house.

"I have a chicken in the slow cooker. Have you plans for dinner?" she asked.

"No."

She smiled a little. His mother had been remiss in not teaching him a more courteous way to speak. He was a very abrupt man. "Would you like to share my supper? I won't make you sing for it."

"I don't have nothing to tell," he replied soberly.

That made her blink. He'd put the criminal interpretation on the word "sing."

Quint saw that he'd surprised her in some way. What had he said? The grammar he'd used was wrong. He should have said he *didn't* have *anything* to tell.

When George went into the kitchen, she expected him to wait in the living room, he'd been so aloof. But he removed his suit jacket, which was of a good make, and folding it correctly, hung it on the back of a chair. Then he unbuttoned his shirt cuffs and rolled up his sleeves. Since it would seem fussy and chiding, she didn't hang his suit coat in the hall closet but left it on the chair. She hadn't expected him to shed the jacket after his stare at her stockinged feet. A complex man, she thought, a puzzle. Who was he?

"I'll set the table," he told her.

Another surprise. After a slow, weighing glance at him, she pulled out dark purple place mats and silver flatware. She showed him where the dishes and glasses

were, but she took the plates and put them on top of
the oven to warm while she baked biscuits.

He set the table carefully, placing the utensils just
so. When she saw that, she went into her bedroom for
her pink begonia and replaced the hardy ivy that sat
on the table in the dim light. The pale pink flowers,
dark purple place mats and pink napkins made the
table nicely festive. And it lifted Georgina's spirits to
make a little more effort.

She prepared cauliflower and broccoli with a cheese
sauce, and some Lambert-family, man-size Texas biscuits. They would be served with the kumquat jam
that her mother had made and which Georgina
hoarded. Now she would share the cherished preserve
with another person for the first time. Saffron was
added to the pale chicken pieces for color, and dinner
was served.

Expecting silence, George had turned the stereo to
an FM station and allowed the man to eat in peace.
Again she sadly marked him off as unreachable. Then
she recalled that without him, Tate might never have
regained her four-year-old son Benjamin, who had
been stolen by Tate's ex-husband. With everyone possible looking for the boy, it was Quint who had found
him. George asked, "Have you seen Benjamin
lately?"

Quint smiled, actually looking into her eyes. "He's
a good kid. Jenny laughs at him. It's nice." Jenny was
Tate's new husband's daughter and a charming twelve-
year-old.

"You pulled off a miracle, finding Benjamin when
no one else could," Georgina said.

Quint dismissed that. "It was a fluke. He'd have been found sometime."

She watched him spread more kumquat jam on a steaming biscuit. "The pictures of Benjamin were a marvelous wedding gift for Tate."

His gaze on Georgina, Quint thought of how he'd planned to use those pictures as a lever to get Bill to back him in expanding his business but how, after his first look at Georgina, Quint had made the pictures a gift to Bill's bride. A man does as he must. He said, "I was glad to do it."

That wasn't true. He'd been shocked by the impulsive giving. That's what a woman could do to a man. This one would wreck him. There he sat in her apartment, in her little dining room, near her, conscious of her, bewitched by her. And he was helpless.

Could he suggest that she sleep with him in order to cure this lovesickness that swamped him? How could he tell her that he needed to make love with her in order to realize she was just like any other female, and that he need not suffer this way? How could he tell her that she was interfering with his life, that he would stare off into space, thinking about her? That she made his nights a torment?

"Have you seen Hillary and Angus lately?" George inquired politely.

"I took over Tate's apartment after she married Bill. Since it's just down the hall from Angus and Hillary's, I see them a lot. Angus is teaching me to sail a boat better, to race."

Georgina thought how interesting that neither of her sisters had mentioned that Quint was in Tate's old apartment. Then George remembered the look Bill had given Angus just before he and Tate left the Lambert house for their honeymoon. It was a warning to Angus to "watch the fox in the chicken coop."

George studied Quint. He wasn't a fox, he wouldn't be sly. He was a dominant wolf. He would order the pack and hunt and fight for them. His pups would be superior. Then she started wondering, what did Quint really do? "What do you do?" But she remembered his question, and changed hers to echo his. "What's your job?"

"I have several businesses."

"Like . . . what?" she encouraged.

"I ship things for organizations." He gestured vaguely. "I collect things for other people. I'm a . . . middleman."

" 'Supply and demand'?"

"Yeah." He stopped with that.

Zero, she thought. He was probably a crook; and that idea depressed her. What else could he be? A "middleman" could be anything. A fence for stolen property? No, he couldn't be that. Angus would know. What did he and Bill know about Quint? Down in Texas, Bill had said vaguely that Quint was an associate. And nothing else had been mentioned. But if they had told Quint to look her up, he must be okay. "Did Hillary and Tate ask you to check on me?"

"No."

No? That let that out. Then why was he here, eating all of her dinner? He would more than likely finish off the chicken, and she would have to find something else for the slow cooker for tomorrow night or eat peanut butter. She sighed as he made further inroads into the jar of kumquat jam. He certainly hadn't come for companionship; so far, his conversation wasn't worth the chicken he was eating, much less her kumquat preserve. But then she became aware of the quivers that shimmied so gently along her nerve ends. They were the aftershocks of the quake her body had sustained at seeing him out in her hallway, waiting for her.

She longed for an excuse to touch him. How could she say "You've eaten up all my chicken and practically all of my jam, so you ought to let me touch you. I'm being driven mad by you. And I think your hands are just beautiful and I want them on me. I want your body." How did a woman go about instigating an affair with such an indifferent, disinterested man? All her life she'd been putting men off. She squinted, trying to remember how men came on to her. She was baffled about how to proceed, so instead she served dessert.

The best she could offer was ice cream. He ate all that, too. The last half-spoonful disappeared between those firm lips. She licked hers, feeling he owed her. First he'd eaten all the chicken, then most of her precious hoarded jam, and now the last of the ice cream.

Quint helped her clear the table and went with her back into the living room. She turned on the news, and they sat and watched it. That is, she watched it; he watched her.

She sat closer to the television than he; therefore he could feast his eyes on her. The sofa was turned so that it angled toward the television. Obviously she would recline on the sofa as she watched the screen.

He saw that she breathed just like any mortal; she blinked her eyes. He was mesmerized to see her tongue touch her lips, and his body was filled with the flood of his desire. She smiled at a commercial. He was breathless, enraptured by her.

He needed her. His breath had become rapid, and it sounded harsh. He was embarrassed by it. Trying not to move too much, he shifted so that he could ease himself. It was exquisite hell to be so close to her. He felt strange... fevered. He was sick with love.

Her small hand moved, and he was awed by its grace. She stretched her back, and he ached to soothe it for her. He wanted his hands on her, his mouth...his body. He barely prevented the groan that built in his throat.

Maybe he should allow the sound its freedom. She'd think he was suffering from indigestion and put him to bed. If he was miserable enough, maybe she'd lie beside him and comfort him by laying her hand on his face. It wouldn't work. If she touched him, he'd explode. So he sat there grimly enduring, silently worshiping her.

In Texas, the very first night of that weekend in November, Angus had managed to tell Quint that the Lamberts weren't ordinary people. They might look and act like anyone else, but their background made the daughters unsuitable for most men.

Quint wasn't stupid. He understood that Angus had seen that he was taken with Georgina, and was warning him off. Angus hadn't meant that Georgina wasn't

suitable for Quint, but the reverse. Georgina was beyond Quint's touch. Had Angus thought that Quint,
from his first glimpse of her, hadn't figured that out
for himself?

But Quint had seen her look at him and smile. A
welcoming smile. Briefly he had wondered if she had
any courage. If she really knew him, could she pitch
all she had and run with him? Could he let her do
that? Of course not. So he'd looked and danced with
her. He'd touched her and felt her against him. But
he'd left her.

What was he doing now, here in her apartment?
Why had he come here to be tortured by her being so
close to him, there, just beyond his hands reach? What
man would do this to himself? *He* would. God, he
would. He narrowed his eyes against the pain inside
him. He longed to touch her, but he didn't move or
speak.

At ten o'clock she turned to him and smiled. "I
have an early day tomorrow. It's been nice to have you
here. Are you staying over?"

"No." He looked at her gloomily. He didn't dare
stick around. He was already shot to hell. He had to
get away and cure himself of her. She could be fatal to
him—the chink in his armor.

She picked up his jacket and handed it to him. He
accepted it. She said, "Tell Bill and Angus 'Hello.'"

He stiffened.

"And give my love to Hillary and Tate and the
kids."

He relaxed a little and nodded, but of course he
wouldn't deliver her messages. If he did, he'd have to

admit he'd gone to Sacramento and seen her. He couldn't do that.

George said nothing more, and he left. She closed the door sadly. There was no chance whatsoever. It was probably just as well he'd left. She sighed dismally.

In the hall, Quint put his hands on her door, bowed his head, and suffered.

The next morning Quint got to the airport and boarded the flight for Chicago, but he got off the plane at the last minute. He made reservations on a later flight, then called Georgina. "My flight was overbooked, and I go later. Can you have lunch with me?"

She laughed—it sounded so deliciously soft in his ear—and said, "Of course."

From a street vendor, Quint bought an umbrella; and in the rain, he waited outside her office building, wondering why he was there.

Georgina came out, greeted him and found he was still tongue-tied with her. She was frustrated, still trying for the feeling of rapport.

Because of the steady rain, there were only a few people walking on the street. They went to the K Street Mall to look in the small shop windows, and they passed an old lady selling fresh flowers displayed on a wide, flat basket.

"Wait here," Quint said to George and left her under the umbrella. He went back to the woman, not noticing that George was following slowly.

She was charmed he would buy her flowers. But then she saw the old lady fill Quint's arms with all of the blossoms, kiss his cheek and walk away. Apparently he'd given the woman enough money for the whole basketful. George was so touched, and she smiled tenderly at him. "You bought them all?"

He avoided the obvious reply. "She ought not be out in the rain. Pick the ones you want and we'll pitch the rest."

But she gave away most of the flowers, and as Quint watched her do that, his heart was filled with her.

From another street vendor, they bought hot dogs and soft drinks for lunch. Then they rode the trolley to Old Town along the Sacramento River. Quint knew when his flight departed without him.

Having stretched Georgina's lunch hour into two, Quint finally signaled for a cab to take her back to her office, and for just a minute she thought he was going to kiss her goodbye. She lifted her mouth a fraction. But he just looked at her in that intense way. Then he said, "Goodbye."

He never called after that, and George languished over the thought of him.

On Christmas Eve at the Lambert house in Texas, Georgina received a large box, by courier, from Chicago. The card read: "Thank you for your hospitality. Finnig."

Inside it was a full-length Russian lynx coat. It was gorgeous. It was the biggest temptation of George's life, so far. She wouldn't let any of her four sisters do anything more than just briefly put it on before she took it back and held it possessively against her body. It wasn't just a coat, it was a symbol of Quint. She kept it for three days, wearing it most of the time—to the sympathy of her smiling, head-shaking family—and then she boxed it back up and reluctantly returned it.

She wrote: "Your mother must have told you a lady can't accept anything so expensive from a gentleman. How lovely it is! Thank you for the compliment, but I must return it to you. I hope your New Year is as you'd like it."

Then, since the note was for Quint, she signed it "Sincerely, Georgina."

In Chicago, Quint put her handwritten note against his chest in anguish and groaned. Just to hold her note! He realized how stupid it was, but knowing that didn't stop him. He looked at her words dozens of times. Her writing was beautiful, the way she was; and exciting, the way she was. And he finally read her reason for returning the coat. His mother? Who the hell *was* his mother?

By then he knew his love for Georgina wasn't something he could put aside. What was he to do? He couldn't bring himself to ask for advice from Georgina's youngest sister Hillary. Her eldest sister Tate was still too remote from him. She was very nice, but she was distracted by having her son back.

Having been warned away from Georgina by them, Quint couldn't reveal his interest in Georgina to either of her brothers-in-law, Bill or Angus. So he went to Marshall Field's department store and asked Customer Service for assistance. They sent him to the gift-suggestions department, where he found a very helpful Mrs. Adams. She was tactful and didn't criticize him. She gave him a list of acceptable presents, taking the time to explain not only what but how much in price and volume. And she added a gentle word or two about restraint. "You've found an old-fashioned girl," she said.

"A lady."

The woman smiled at Quint and agreed. "A lady."

"So I can send her flowers."

When Georgina returned to Sacramento, she received a bouquet of flowers. On the card was carefully written: "Thank you for a very nice evening. Quintus Finnig."

But Georgina didn't hear anything else from him. After the gift of the fur coat, she'd thought perhaps his visit to Sacramento wasn't as casual as it had appeared. Maybe she hadn't been tactful enough in returning his coat. Had she hurt his feelings? Hurt male feelings weren't something she'd especially worried about before then.

After a week into the New Year, Georgina arranged to have a friend over for supper who was interested in analyzing handwriting. Georgina had photocopied Quint's note but not his signature.

As soon as Charlene came in the door of Georgina's apartment—-before she'd even removed her raincoat—Georgina thrust the note into her hand. "What do you think?" she asked.

"Good grief, George, give me a minute. This is a science. It needs attention. I can't give you a quick judgment. Who is this guy?"

"I can't say at this time. I don't know him very well. He sent me a lynx coat for Christmas, and I sent it back. So he sent me flowers."

"A *lynx* coat? A real lynx? And you sent it *back*?"

"Come on, Charlene, you know good and well I couldn't keep it."

"Why didn't you tell him it got lost in the mail? You could have slit the bottom of the box and put in a note saying: 'If the bottom of the box is slit, someone stole the coat.'"

"Don't think I wasn't tempted."

They sat down to eat, and Charlene studied the few words all through a delicious pot-roast cooked with potatoes, onions and carrots, just like Charlene's mother used to make before she'd gotten a microwave oven. George had prepared it specially, as a bribe.

As the meal progressed without a word from Charlene, George became restless. Finally Charlene declared, "In a snap analysis—this is so carefully written, it isn't the real writing. He's contriving a facade. That fact says something about him. He's trying to impress you. But the coat proved that. Who is he? Do I know him? Is it Phillip? I've been wracking my brain figuring who you know out here who has that much money."

"Quit guessing, and tell me what you see in his writing."

"Okay. He's very strong and devious."

"I already knew that."

"What you really want to know is if he's interested in you and if he's a good lover."

"Charlene!" George was indignant.

"Well, isn't that right?"

"Yes, but it sounds so crass said out loud that way."

"That's not being crass, buttercup, that's being lustful. And I must say I never in this world thought I'd ever hear of Georgina Lambert being—*gasp!*—lustful over a man."

"We all have our Achilles' heels."

"Honey, we're not talking heels here," Charlene said suggestively.

But George, mindful of how little she did know about Quint, wasn't at all sure that they *weren't* talking about a *heel*. There was something very smoky about Quintus Finnig.

Two

In the following dark, rainy days of Sacramento's winter, George pined and acted strangely like a woman who had been abandoned by some foolishly stupid man. Since she couldn't believe her actual emotions were involved, and since it was the first time she'd ever experienced anything remotely similar, she rather wallowed in the unusual melancholy feelings.

George's friends frowned at her and then at one another, trying to fathom what on earth ailed her. Charlene was questioned, but she had no real knowledge of who or what, since she hadn't seen the note's signature. She could only shrug in such a telling way that everyone knew she knew, but was being steadfast and loyal in pretending not to know anything.

In her office, George stared unseeingly at a picture of a window on her windowless wall, and was struck by such a basic solution that she was amazed. She called her brother-in-law, Bill, at his office in Chicago.

"George?" he asked in surprise. "What's the matter?"

"Nothing's wrong," she assured him. "How is everyone? Everything okay?"

"Yes, sure. What's up with you?"

"I just wanted to talk to you about... I suppose this is a poor time. I can call back later."

"No, no. I've all the time in the world for you. Tell me about whatever it is."

She blurted, "I'd like to know about Finnig."

"Why?"

"Uh, well, you know. Down home you said he was an associate, and I just wondered what you might know about him."

"I said 'associate' because he was helping look for Benjamin. I really don't know anything about Finnig. Angus cleared him for me. Why are you asking about him? You stay away from him."

"I'm in Sacramento. I'm nowhere even *close* to Chicago."

"Has he been out there?"

"Why do you ask that?" she asked, evading his question.

"George, why are you asking about Finnig?"

"No reason. I was just thinking about him and—"

"Did he send you another coat?"

"No! Quit being paranoid, Bill. I'm sorry I called and—"

"No, no, no. I'm glad to talk to you any time." He slowed down and spoke less intensely. "It's just that I worry that you're interested in Finnig. I think any involvement, in any kind of relationship with him, would present too many problems. I'm not sure about his background, at all. He isn't connected with any family that I know about. I seriously believe he is completely unsuitable. Is that what you want to know?"

"No," Georgina replied with a touch of irritation.

"Then what?"

"I was just idle for a while. I've been bored and Tate's phone was busy."

They both knew she was lying.

"Well, I'm glad you called. When are you going to teach me to speak properly in front of an audience?"

"Who needs to teach a hound to suck eggs?" She chose the country expression, knowing Bill understood what it meant.

He laughed, and they hung up soon after, without referring to Quint again.

But later she called Angus. He too was surprised to hear from her and he, too, used the word *unsuitable* to describe Quint Finnig, adding that his background and people were untraceable.

Then Georgina called her dad. After a more cautious approach, beginning with talking about Benjamin and going through other family members, she asked, "Do you remember the man who brought the pictures of Benjamin to Bill and Tate?"

"Yeah, sugar."

Georgina heard the subtle change in her father's voice and wondered if Bill or Angus had called him and warned him that she'd asked about Finnig. Of course not. She was the one who was getting paranoid. "What did you think of him?"

"Well . . . I'm not sure I paid him that much attention. Why?"

"Oh, he was just different. I was thinking about him, and you never did actually say anything about him that I could recall. Uh, did Momma say anything to you about him?"

Her papa heard all the "hims" in her questioning. "I believe she mentioned how inappropriate it was of him to send you that raccoon coat and—"

"Raccoon! Papa, that was lynx!"

"Now, now. How was I to tell? We hardly have any of them kind around these parts." He was teasing her, and he went on talking and visiting. George had hung up before she realized her daddy had never offered any opinion of Quint Finnig.

Finally, in desperation, she called Sling. He wasn't yet kin, but he would be as soon as George's sister Fredricka could convince him that he was interested in her. Sling had met Quint that weekend of the weddings and would be able to give an unprejudiced opinion.

"Hey, George, you finally calling me, too?" Sling's deep voice asked.

"What do you mean by that?"

"From what I understand, you've called both your brothers-in-law and your daddy. And now me. You want to know what I think about Finnig, right?"

Georgina groaned. "Good grief."

"Well, I'll tell you. I'd hire him like a shot."

"Thanks, Sling."

"You're welcome. But hiring a man to work for you and recommending him to a woman are two different things. I doubt he's suitable."

"Oh."

"Understand?" Sling pushed it.

"Yes."

Having run out of people with whom she could talk about Quint, George looked up the word *unsuitable* in the dictionary. It said: "unfitting." The parts wouldn't fit. She and Quint would find it difficult to meld into an easy relationship.

Not even the dictionary communicated what she wanted to hear.

Whether or not Quintus Finnig was "suitable" really didn't matter after all. He never called or wrote or sent her any more fur coats. The days passed, and Georgina's life went on as it normally would. She began to date Martin. He was intelligent, nice looking, with a good sense of humor. And he was suitable.

She'd met him one day during lunch with Charlene and several other friends. She hadn't really paid much attention to him.

So she was surprised when Martin had called her and asked if she'd like to go out with him. She'd declined that offer and the next one. But after coming back from Christmas holidays in sunny Texas to the doldrums of California's rainy season, George had agreed to a date.

It was a day or so after that when she mentioned it to Charlene. "Remember the Martin that we m—"

"You went out with him," Charlene stated in a very quiet voice.

"Yes. Just to a film. We had a nice time."

"Did you go to bed with him?"

"Good God, Charlene! You know perfectly well—"

"I know! I know you don't, but he could change any woman's mind."

"We went with three other couples," Georgina explained, feeling exasperated.

She was so sunk in her own grieving for that stupid Quintus Finnig that she almost failed to notice such betraying clues from Charlene. Then she felt a nudge to pay more attention to what was wrong with her friend. After she'd recovered from Quint a little, she would give Charlene more time and figure out what ailed her. It was probably some man, Georgina decided; and who could solve men?

Since Georgina passed on single dating, Martin snared her with a group date for a rainy day. She laughed. He'd been clever enough to gather other people, and dressed for the weather, they went hiking. They were all a ghastly mess, and they had a marvelous time.

His next lure was a dance at a park pavilion, and after that, there was a gourmet-dinner cooking party.

That was chaos, with everyone having to reach around and over everyone else in Martin's tiny kitchen.

Georgina opened the door for the late-arriving Charlene, who brought a bottle of wine in a wicker basket. The bottle just happened to be a very expensive one that Martin loved. Charlene appeared surprised to hear that, but when Martin lifted the bottle high and leaned to kiss Charlene's cheek, she sank back against the counter and seemed immobilized for a time. No one but George saw that Charlene was under some stress and George felt another nudge to find out what ailed her friend pretty soon—after she got over Quintus Finnig and her feeling of having lost something very important to her.

But she didn't get Quintus Finnig solved. He haunted her dreams and any idle time. The thought of him was always there. It was really very sad.

A welcome break came for George in the last week in January. Along with her four sisters and two brothers-in-law, George went to the Lambert family home to celebrate their mother's birthday. Those milestones had become precious. Mrs. Lambert claimed to be Jack Benny's ageless thirty-nine, but that made her only four years older than her first child, and there were some blats of disbelief.

"Since Tate's pregnant—" Hillary began.

"Good heavens, Hillary—" Tate protested.

Variations of "What?" from the others drowned out the rest of her denial. Bill and Tate exchanged a laughing look.

At one point when the five sisters were lounging around, George mentioned very casually, "Has anyone seen anything of...what was his name? Quint?"

"I remember him! Is he still around loose?" Roberta asked.

"What do you mean, 'loose'?" Georgina asked.

"Not in prison." Roberta laughed.

Then the other three sisters began to talk all at once, and the subject was lost.

During that weekend Georgina found an opportunity to ask Bill very offhandedly, "Uh, have you seen Quint around?"

Bill said, "No."

Georgina didn't believe him for a minute.

It was more difficult to corner Angus. But she was persistent, and she did manage. She tried to be casual about it. "Oh, by the way, have you seen anything of, what's his name, uh, Quint?"

"No," Angus said. "He's not someone you should be asking after."

"Oh, for Pete's sake—" she started to say, then stopped her tongue. She'd almost betrayed the fact that Bill had replied similarly.

All through the birthday weekend, Georgina thought about Quint, and her moist eyes were accepted as the result of watching precious old family movies and listening to hilarious old jokes. No one knew it wasn't sentimental nostalgia that puddled her eyes, but that she was grieving for an unsuitable man. Not only unsuitable, but unobtainable. It was a hopeless situation.

The weekend passed, and the rest of the family had to hurry back to jobs and their own homes. Even Fred worked while she waited for Sling to come to his senses. So George hung around and allowed her parents to spoil her rotten.

She finally decided that the real lure of Quintus Finnig was the fact that he *was* unsuitable. There was an obstinate streak in Lamberts that did egg them on, occasionally, into doing stupid things.

At family reunions, Lamberts bragged about some of those ridiculous strivings undertaken against all good sense: cattle drives in Indian territory; tangles with gunslingers, bankers, railroad men. All sorts of opposition—and they'd won!

Of course, no one ever said a thing about the ones who must have failed. Still, the ones who'd survived were George's ancestors. Those who'd failed had been lost to the genetic pool, so she had to be of the winners, those who had taken their chances and won.

She realized she was thinking utter nonsense. Not one female ancestor had gone out to win the heart of a highwayman. Or if she had, no one had mentioned it.

If George went to Chicago and snared Quintus Finnig, would her name drop out of the family tree? Fall and rot on the ground? He just might be worth it.

How could she go up there to Chicago and find him? Neither Bill nor Angus would give her any help at all. Perhaps she could call him. So she went to the library, but they didn't have a Chicago telephone directory. "We've never felt the need for one." The librarian was a little defensive when George was so disappointed. "We don't have one for Paris, France, either. You can call Information, you know."

She tried that from a pay phone. "We have no phone listed for that party," the operator replied.

A man like Quint probably lived with forty women and didn't have time to answer the phone.

A few days later, Fred asked, "How long are you staying, George? How can you take off this much time?"

Irritated, George groused, "I've only been here five days. I'm not scheduled for anything, so there's no pressing need for me to go back."

"Are you okay? Is there anything bothering you? Do you need any help?"

That was pretty strong from Fred, who was the least decisive of the Lambert sisters. For her to volunteer help, to even notice that someone else might need help, was really rather amazing. Chagrined, George replied, "I'm fine."

"You don't act too fine. Are you zonked over Quintus?" Fred looked very concerned.

"Of course not! Why would you ask something so silly?"

"You called Sling. No woman calls an attractive man like Sling for his opinion about another man, unless that other man means something to her."

"Sling was just like everyone else. He too said Quint's unsuitable."

"Pay attention. Sling is about the most tolerant man I've ever known. If he says Quint's unsuitable, then you should believe him."

Georgina smiled sadly. "Not only Sling, but Papa, Bill and even Angus."

"You really hunted for an affirmative response." Fred reached over and hugged Georgina. As she sat back and looked at her younger sister, she saw the tears. "Oh, George, maybe you ought to see him again. Maybe that coat dazzled you."

"Not the coat. The man."

"Oh, honey, what are we to do about you? You must have a terrible case on that man. And in just that brief time at Tate's marriage!"

"Well, I did see him one other time. Don't you dare tell. He came to Sacramento, but we hardly even talked. He scolded me for not having my key ready and he told me to have the one branch of the tree that's outside my window cut off, and he ate all my chicken and never touched me." She started gulping down sobs.

"He came to Sacramento? Did he stay with you?"

"No. He just criticized me and left."

"But he sent you the coat."

"But he hasn't called me or come to see me or anything."

"It's probably just as well. Golly, George, even Papa said he's unsuitable?"

"Actually, Papa avoided giving an opinion."

Fred nodded with understanding. "He's never said anything one way or the other about Sling, either. But Papa has friends all over Texas who've been offering me all sorts of tempting jobs that are a distance from Sling. I can't take that as any vote of confidence in Sling."

"Has Sling guessed you have a brain?"

"I've never pushed the fact."

That distracted Georgina. "Why not?"

"Sling has never shown any particular fascination with brains."

"In marriage there is always the possibility that there will be the urge to have children, and intelligence in offsprings is a consideration.

"Do you mean that Sling thinks I'm a bubblehead?" Fred frowned at George.

"I have no idea."

Fred considered that possibility. "I may surprise him."

After a moment's silence, George asked, "What do you suggest I do about Quint?"

Fred looked at her for a long time, then she said gently, "Three men, whose opinions you respect, have told you that he's unsuitable."

George could think of no reply.

So George went back to Sacramento and soberly faced the fact that, for the third time, she had given up on ever seeing Quint again or knowing him better. Or loving him. If three was a charm, then this third relinquishment was a final letting-go. George grieved.

Martin called. "I heard you were back in town. How did the visit go?"

Since she was feeling so lost, she especially appreciated his call. They talked for a while, and it was pleasant.

When George thought about it, she realized Martin was a nice guy. He was courteous; he let her know that he liked her. He didn't just sit around eating all her chicken and kumquat jam; he actually spoke to her. And he didn't criticize her or tell her to cut off the tree branch outside her window. He met people openly, was willing to be friends, and didn't look around all the time as if he expected someone was going to attack him.

Martin seemed honest. No woman would have to wonder if he was on the right side of the law or have to call around to people who had dubious opinions of him.

Martin had kissed George. He did it nicely; really very pleasantly. And he touched her—not lingeringly, but nicely. He didn't treat her as if she had the plague and didn't dare get near her. He let her know that he liked her and made it clear he wanted to be with her, and he never acted as if he'd been forced to endure her company, submitting to it until he could leave at the first opportunity.

Everybody liked Martin. No one warned that he was unsuitable. People enjoyed being with him, and no one had tried to get him to leave any gathering.

And George knew Charlene liked Martin so well that she colored a little and couldn't seem to be quite natural around him; but Charlene was too loyal a friend to deliberately flirt with him. However, Charlene did touch him without realizing she was doing it. It just seemed as if Charlene's hands were drawn to Martin, and she was always surprised and a little embarrassed when she found they were on him. George didn't mind.

It was the fact that she didn't mind that made her pause and think about her own friendship with Martin. George finally understood that Martin was getting ready to settle down, and he was considering her. Did she want Martin? The answer was: only as a friend.

While she was still considering how to tell Martin she was only a friend, Susan, a rather casual acquaintance, suggested a couple of days skiing. George snapped at it. "Good. I need to get away." She completely ignored the fact that she'd been out of town twice in five weeks.

She had to break a date with Martin. He wanted to go along skiing, but George said none of their other friends was going this time. That should allow Martin to realize she considered him only as part of the group.

Her boss wasn't at all thrilled. "Hell, George, you were just down in Texas." He frowned at her. But he was a sensitive man and understood Georgina was under some strain, so he said kindly, "Go ahead. But you're out of vacation time. This'll be docked from your paycheck."

"Right."

George borrowed her friend Frances's pink ski outfit. "You get one snag in it and you replace it. Got that?" Frances warned.

"There's one here on the fanny."

"Noted."

"How about this stain on the knee?" Georgina inquired, holding up the soiled part.

"You can hardly see it."

"Hah! If I hadn't pointed it out, when I get back you'd accuse me of rolling around in the mud with some guy. How *did* that stain get there? There isn't any mud where you can ski. Come on, tell me."

"Wouldn't you like to know." Frances turned up her nose. Then she said with a sigh, "When my nephew came visiting, he wanted to sleep in the backyard. If I wasn't his favorite aunt, I'd have told him to forget it. But since he assured me that I am, I couldn't say no. I didn't dare allow him out there in the dark night all alone, and I froze, so I put that on."

"I'll mend this rip under the right arm," George said sweetly.

"Oh, good grief!" Frances burst out laughing, and George hugged her.

The day before the trip, George had lunch with Charlene. "I've never been very good on skis. If I break my neck, you can have Martin." George looked up to share a grin and was surprised by the most appalled look on Charlene's face. "What's the matter?"

"Oh, George, I don't want you dead, I—"

George was astonished. Charlene wanted Martin? Like blips, the memories of Charlene with Martin went through George's mind and realization finally came that Charlene was taken with him! "Well, for Pete's sake! You've got a crush on Martin!"

"I don't really want you dead."

George laughed. "He's a nice guy. Ask him to supper while I'm gone."

"You wouldn't mind?"

"We're just a part of the group. No romance."

"I don't want you dead," Charlene repeated.

George smiled at her friend. "Don't worry about me. Nothing could possibly happen to me. I take good care of myself."

Three

Susan had chosen the place where they would ski. Since the trip was Susan's idea, George couldn't protest too much. She knew the lodge was exclusive. To go there, one had to be sponsored by a member. Susan had that contact. "Why there?" George had asked. "I hear that's a posh place. I only have Frances's pink ski suit, and it'll look like I'm trying to be cutesy."

Susan looked at George from head to toe and replied with some patience, "Such an impression would be very temporary. You'll be fine."

On the way to the lodge, George noted how the highway plow had cleared away the snow, blowing it past both sides of the roads leaving two walls of snow that were two cars high. But the roadbed was still

snow-packed. The lodge was in the Sierra Nevada
Mountains, northeast of Sacramento and almost to
the Nevada border. It was north and west of Lake Ta-
hoe. The area was part of the national forest preserve, and the mountains were awesome. George, who
had never been in that particular region, was very impressed.

Built on a level below the ski trails, the lodge was
solid and rugged looking on the outside. The interior
continued the rustic feeling, but it was obviously a
luxurious place. Georgina realized that the people who
came there could be confident that the other guests
would be of the same echelon socially and finan-
cially, and that there would be acquaintances and ex-
periences in common.

It wasn't until the two women had arrived at the
lodge that Georgina discovered Susan had arranged to
meet her friend Mike there. So George went out to
tackle the slopes by herself.

She was surprised by the number of men who appeared with her on the practice slopes. Their ease on
skis clearly marked them as too advanced to be begin-
ners. Then she realized she was prey.

It took her most of the first day and half of the next
to convince the interested males that although she was
wearing such an eye-catching outfit, she wasn't a ski-
lodge groupie. She tried to turn them off by saying
"The suit color was originally red—it faded."

But they responded with "You burned it out,
right?"

So she tried "The color is misleading. I borrowed it
because it's warm."

"Need warming, huh?"

Since Susan was being so friendly with Mike, and she was there with Georgina, it made Georgina appear to be of the same ilk. But since George kept insisting she wasn't looking for anyone, by the end of the second day the loose and hunting men began to leave her alone.

After lunch on the third day, George went out on the terrace with Susan and Mike. Most of the guests were there, sitting at tables in the sun, sipping hot chocolate and resting before returning to the slopes.

Georgina looked around. There were probably close to seventy guests, most of whom were men. Georgina had noticed that the men met, talked and circulated so that in an evening they had conversations with a good number of people—serious talks, not the smiling, nodding kind between strangers. She thought it was odd for so many people to be at a holiday lodge who not only were acquainted, but appeared to do business with one another.

George had noted there was an unmarked door into which men disappeared after dinner at night. She wondered if there was gambling. Or was it business? What sort?

These people all had the facade of new money. They "belonged," and they had the confidence of those who had it made.

So it was rather a jolt to the individuals lolling in such security, when their serene silence was broken by the sound of a powerful machine approaching. It wasn't the high whine of a snowmobile, but the deep growl of a motorcycle.

From the men's small movements, it was obvious that territorial hackles were stirred. Georgina thought it must be a little disconcerting for them to feel the primitive rise of hairs on the spines of their well-kept bodies.

As if in disbelief, heads slowly turned toward the road that would eventually reveal the intruder. Who would be so stupid as to ride a motorcycle up snow-covered mountain roads and to that particular lodge? Talk about a misfit—a hexagon intruding into a conventionally rounded watering hole.

On the far side of the terrace, one of the men slowly rose to his feet to lean a hip against the rail and very casually light a cigarette. Georgina smiled. Men were so predictable. It was as if the railing around the terrace had become a thorn-bush wall barring the stranger, and they were all gathered behind it to defend their territory. It would be interesting to see how they would handle this intruder who was coming into their bailiwick.

The suspense was building nicely, Georgina thought. Now, no one spoke. They were all concentrating on the approaching threat. Now, why did she label the sound a "threat"? She glanced around, turning her head fractionally. The guests were no longer relaxed, not even the women. The men seemed braced, but the women appeared excited. Hands reached to smooth hair, lips were moistened. These pampered, coddled women were stimulated by a rough sound?

What about her? Was she stimulated? Georgina examined her senses and decided it had to be a very dull day for an intrusive motorcycle to elicit this much attention. She discreetly stretched her nice body. Skiing was fine, but after three days, it stopped being exciting.

The roar burst from around the last bend in the road, and the monster came into sight. The watchers moved in jerks, stretching necks, turning, rising.

The man on the cycle came closer, throttling down with a rudely loud noise. He made an exciting picture, riding that machine. It was very much like watching a jousting knight. A knight of the road?

According to her admittedly limited observation, those "knights" got off their cycles to reveal potbellies and soft muscles. They rode distances, drank beer while they rested, then rode the distances back. But this one was different. He was a commanding figure and looked as if he could handle anything, including all of the spectators.

He wore black leather—boots, gloves, a fur-lined jacket—and a black helmet with a blackened visor. He looked formidable. A lick of something like fear went through Georgina and surprised her, it was so sexual. She smiled to herself in derision.

The unwelcome visitor eased the quietly throbbing motorcycle to the cleared dry spot by the steps and stopped. Switching off the motor, he sat for a minute in the sudden silence, slowly pulling off his gloves and laying them on the machine. He then rose, lifting a booted leg free of the cycle to stand sideways, his feet planted.

He was wide shouldered and had a flat stomach. His hips were lean and his movements slow. With the black helmet, he looked deadly.

George studied him, reminding herself he was just a man. He appeared to scan them, and it seemed as if his black-screened gaze came to her and stopped. She felt a very strange prickling up her back, under her arms and over her breasts as her nipples tightened. She found her breath was affected. How strange.

His head was bent forward, and as he moved to the cycle, his boots scraped the asphalt, making a sound that broke the stillness. Slowly he lifted his helmet from his head, hesitated, then lowered it to his chest, revealing his face. His straight dark brown hair fell across his forehead, and his thick brows were straight lines.

George gasped. "Finnig?"

It was only later that she recalled the sound of glass shattering at her word.

Quint Finnig's glance went briefly to the tinkling of the breaking glass, but immediately came back to Georgina. His face appeared to soften though it actually didn't change, and he looked into her blue eyes as if he was drinking in the sight of her.

George thought that he was different from the last time she'd seen him. Drawn to him, she rose and walked to the top of the steps. "Are you here?" Immediately she thought, what a perfectly stupid question—of course he was there! But it was so...astonishing. Finnig in that place?

Quint said, "Georgina." From the bottom of the steps, he studied her to see if she was still the way he remembered. She was. It wasn't his yearning that had clothed her in magic. She *was* magic. He'd never believed a woman could affect him in such a way.

He dragged his stare from her and looked around at the mesmerized audience. They appeared grim and unwelcoming, as if they were expecting him to carry her off.

He sent his glance down her nice body. "Do you have anything to wear that's warm enough for riding with me?" He noted how his words carried in that intense stillness.

She tilted her head back and laughed. It sounded delicious and seemed to promise that whatever adventure he'd brought, she'd be a part of it. He grinned but he saw that no one else did.

Her laugh seemed to infect the men with an aversion to him. There were automatic rejecting movements, as if only the thin veneer of civilization prevented the group from storming forth and disposing of such an intruder. He smiled again and he heard the surprised intakes of several breaths.

Georgina stretched an innocent hand out to him. "Come inside where we can talk. Have you seen Tate lately? How is Benjamin? What's going on? Why are you here?"

That question again. That's what Angus and Bill had asked him last November when he'd turned up in Texas, uninvited. He put his foot on the bottom step and two of the men stood up. He gave them a dismissive glance and took the next step, smiling. He was used to being challenged. He knew this kind of men, he knew how to handle them. They would back down. He took another step.

Georgina thought he was magnificent. What other man could face down that whole terrace of strangers as if they didn't matter?

Then he surprised her. As he came to the last step— their faces were almost level but he still had to lower his eyes to look into hers—he smiled at her. He really was different; more intense or something. He was *conscious* of her. Why hadn't he shown this much interest in her at her apartment? Her nerves were in a shimmy, and she couldn't do anything except stare back.

A tingling swept through her body. It was so sexual. She wanted him. Astonishing. All those men there in that place had had no effect on her at all, but when Finnig came, she became weak-kneed and pliant. Why?

Being together in the big Lambert house for the weekend with all those other people, and sharing her chicken dinner just before Christmas, didn't make them friends. Why was she so attracted to this man? He was like no other. But then she smiled at him.

He took the last step onto the terrace and loomed over her. He took her hand. It was a declaration of possession. By that simple act, he'd claimed Georgina as his. He glanced around in challenge. No one moved.

"Come inside," Georgina repeated, and tightened her hand on his grip.

"Ge-o-o-r-r-g-ge . . ." It was Susan's bid for attention.

But Georgina found herself rejecting not only the intrusion but her nickname. She said, "We'll be inside." She tugged on Quint's hand with a possessiveness of her own, and moved toward the door.

The people made some responsive movements that could have been protests to Quint's intrusion. But his glance turned their gestures into motions of getting ready to leave for the slopes. It was as if they couldn't sit still any longer. The men spoke to one another as they stood or stretched, and were being very self-consciously male.

One man angled his steps so that he met the pair at the door. "Where are you from?" he asked Quint in a seemingly friendly way.

"Who wants to know?" Quint stared at him stonily.

"Well—" the man laughed with a false heartiness "—I heard her call you Finnig, and I believe I know of a man by that name."

"It's not me." Finnig reached past Georgina, opened the door and crowded her through it.

"That wasn't very friendly," she chided him.

"Why should I be friendly to him?" he asked, surprised.

"It's just part of being courteous."

He smiled down at her, watching her, but he also looked around the lobby and into the adjoining rooms, noting everything. No one was missed in his examination.

She led him into a small alcove. She never once dreamed of inviting him into her room. She'd been strictly raised. Her room did have soft chairs, but it also held a big bed and that made it too personal a place to invite a strange man. So she seated herself in the alcove. "Would you like to take off your jacket?"

"Do you have something else you can wear? Long johns? Come ride with me. I've got a helmet for you. It's pretty down the road."

She recalled that the two other times she'd been with Quint he'd spoken this carefully, as if he planned his words. "I have a car, let's go in that," she replied.

"No. Come with me."

This time he was as aggressive, as positive as she'd wanted him to be. She laughed. "Oh-h-h, all right. I'll be back in a minute."

He watched her leave, then transferred his gaze to the man by the door who'd questioned him. Finnig gave him a hard, dismissing look and then ignored him. But the man approached him. Finnig faced him, his feet planted as he slowly unzipped his jacket in a very intimidating way.

With an ingratiating smile, the man spoke. "You seem so familiar, and I'm curious who you are."

"You gotta know about curious. You don't know me."

"How can you be sure?"

Finnig said, "If you did, I'd know."

"Perhaps we have friends in common."

"I'm not looking to . . . chat." Finnig made the last word sound final. Dismissively, he turned away, shrugging out of his jacket.

The man hesitated, not wanting to leave but clearly needing to question further.

Finnig turned and pretended to be surprised to see the man still hanging around. He lifted one eyebrow, then snubbed the man by turning away, picking up a magazine and sitting down, his head bent over the open pages.

"I'm Roscoe Morris. I know your name."

Finnig took a deep breath before he looked up with excruciating patience. He gave the man a long, silent stare and no help at all.

"Does my name ring a bell?" Morris smiled.

"No."

"I know I know you. What's your full name? Where's your home?"

Finnig allowed the words to hang in the air for some time, then he said, carefully, "You're being... tiresome." The word was carefully chosen.

"Oh. I beg your pardon. But I know you."

"I don't mind if you do," he replied with indifference.

"But—"

Finnig went back to the magazine, ignoring the man who stood restlessly before him.

Georgina returned, a little flushed by her hurrying back to Quint. She grinned at finding him still there. She wore thermal long underwear and a mohair sweater under her ski clothes. She'd wound a scarf around her throat and carried her shoulder bag.

Finnig rose and pulled his jacket back on as the man appealed to Georgina. "I know I know him. Where's he from?"

Georgina wasn't stupid. Finnig didn't want to talk to this pushy man. With a straight face, she replied, "From out of the west, he came riding—riding. . . ."

Quint grinned. He'd read the poem, it was "The Highwayman". She thought him a highwayman? Maybe she wasn't far off the mark.

He took her hand, and they walked past the hapless man, out of the room and the building and down the steps to the big black machine, which stood there, waiting for them.

Finnig helped Georgina put on the extra helmet to be sure it fit right and was comfortable. He showed her how to plug in the two-way radio so that despite the sound of the rushing wind and the noise of the machine, they could talk as they went down the road.

"We can talk?" She looked up at him.

"Yes." His eyes watched her intently.

She thought of riding with her body close in back of his, her knees on either side of his lean hips, while she listened to his voice in her ear. She was so acutely conscious of him. All her nerves danced sinuously because he was there by her, and that astonished her, but dormant places stirred and she was shocked.

She gave him a quick look. His brown eyes seemed to hold yellow flames, and he appeared to know exactly what she was feeling. He couldn't possibly know, could he? Good grief. Surely he couldn't know her body's reaction to him. Blushing, she settled the helmet. Then she remembered all the things the men in her family had said of this stranger, and she had some qualms.

She felt the strongest urge to take off her helmet and toss it at him. While he caught it, she could run up the steps, into the lodge, slam the door and lean against it.

It wouldn't do any good. This new Finnig would just put the helmet back on the machine, come up the steps, effortlessly open the door and take her back outside. He would act like a man claiming a woman.

Had he come here to claim her?

She considered that prospect as those dormant places within her began to heat. So did her cheeks. He couldn't possibly be interested in her in *that* way, not after only seeing her in that mob of relatives down in Texas, and in that zero time in Sacramento. No man could possibly become interested in a woman after two such blah times. Could he?

Of course, they'd danced in Texas after the wedding. He'd danced with her mother and Bill's mother. He'd danced with all the ladies. And the giggling little girls. And her. He'd danced all the slow dances...with her. He'd pulled her close against that large, hard body of his and held her there as they'd moved to the slow rhythms, brushing against each other, their bodies gently rubbing. His breathing had been uneven. His hands had been so hot. Not sweaty, but burning. And he had radiated heat. They hadn't said much of anything. But while everyone else had called her George, Quint had called her Georgina.

Standing there at the foot of the lodge steps, she felt she was reading more into this chance meeting than could possibly be there. She asked him curiously, ''Why are you here?''

There was that question again. He allowed his gaze to roam over her perfect face and come to rest on her mouth. "I was just passing through."

She'd been a bit wide-eyed, but at his reply, her lashes drooped and she scoffed. "Down a private road that dead-ends at a lodge?"

He glanced over at the building. "Hardly a lodge, a place like that."

"How do you know that?"

"I know of the guy that owns it." Quint put on his own helmet and closed the black-tinted visor, effectively disappearing.

"You know Kennerly?"

"The guy that owns him," Quint clarified.

Startled, she stared hard at his covered face. "He's . . . owned?"

"Yeah. You oughtn't go places you don't know about."

"Everybody comes here." She gestured to the area. "It's a meeting place."

"That's true. People come here from all over the country. It's quiet, well run and—"

"Ladies ought not to be here." Quint was adamant.

"Why not?"

"Something could happen to them."

Four

Something could happen to her? What did Quint mean by that? Georgina laughed a little, recalling how the harsh sounds of his approaching motorcycle had held the people on the terrace mesmerized, and how she'd foolishly imagined the rider was dangerous. She looked up at Quint Finnig. Was he dangerous? She turned her gaze aside, again uncertain.

He must have misread her, because he tried to comfort her. "I'm taking you away from here." He put her purse in the luggage box, closed her visor and showed her how to get on the little tandem seat. There was a backrest against the luggage box. It was quite comfortable. Then he straddled the machine in front of her. "Hold on to me," he said over his shoulder.

His bulk blocked her view ahead, and she put her hands on his wide, strong shoulders. Because she'd never been on a motorcycle, she was very interested and paid close attention to what Quint did. He started the machine, revved it, moved it just a little, then accelerated. Lifting his booted feet on to the rests, he guided them into a wide, smooth circle, then eased the machine down the road.

In her delight, Georgina laughed softly in Finnig's ear. Then in his rearview mirror, he saw Morris and two other men hurry out onto the terrace to watch them leave. One ran back inside. That was all Quint needed to know. He went down the hill out of sight from the lodge, lifted a hand high and waved it in a circle. Then he concentrated on the road.

"Who'd you wave to?" Georgina asked.

"A friend."

His voice sounded just as she'd feared it would. Her toes curled in her boots while her erogenous zones shivered. Riding through the snowy winter landscape on a motorcycle she could be turned on? Incredible.

There was no traffic on that small road north of Interstate 80. As he drove along, Quint commented on the landscape. "This is different from Chicago." He spoke the words carefully, as he had before. Again his comment was brief.

"Different from Texas, too," she replied.

"Are you warm enough?"

"So far."

"We'll be there soon."

"Where?"

"You'll see." That was all he said.

Her qualms returned. "Where are we going?"

"I'll explain later. I'll take care of you."

What did he mean by that? It sounded as if they weren't just taking a ride but going to some *place*.

She began to chide herself for having an overactive imagination, but she suddenly, vividly remembered that her sister Tate had been snatched briefly by some unknowns in Chicago last summer, and Quintus Finnig had helped find her. Was he with the mysterious, unnamed kidnappers? But he had had people looking for Tate. He couldn't be involved with those kind of men. Could he? He'd said the lodge was not a place for women. How did he know that?

He was so attuned to her, guessing her confusion, that he said, "It's okay. No problem. We'll get there soon."

"Where?" she asked again.

"Don't worry about it. Look at that drop. You go down that, and nobody'd ever find you."

What did he mean by that? Her fingers let go of his shoulders.

He felt her withdrawal. "Hold on."

"I can balance okay."

"I need you to touch me so I'll know how you're shifting."

Now, how could she get off this machine? There was no way. She'd have to fling a leg over his head and he'd surely notice that, she thought ruefully.

Why wouldn't he tell her where they were going? Again she considered that her brothers-in-law had been uneasy about Finnig when he had shown up uninvited in Texas. Uninvited was how he'd arrived at her apartment in Sacramento, and uninvited was exactly the way he'd shown up there at the lodge. He'd simply arrived. And in front of all those people, he had acted as if he was her old friend.

Who knew this Chicago man was here in California? Who realized that he might not take her back to the lodge?

Susan had asked to meet him. But Georgina had been so eager to be with him, with her nerves all dancing in excitements, that she'd ignored the opportunity for Susan to get a good look at him and know his full name. How many Finnigs were there in the world? But no one knew who this one was.

If Georgina didn't return to the lodge, no one would worry. They'd think she'd just gone off with him. Susan wouldn't question it at all. Georgina had left of her own free will.

Finnig was from Chicago. Everyone knew what a wild place Chicago was. It had all sorts of people. Gangsters. What did Georgina know that someone else needed to know so badly that they would send a Chicago man clear out to a remote ski lodge in the Sierra Nevada Mountains?

After a time she said aloud, "We've come a long way."

"We're almost there," he replied. "We had to get far enough away from the lodge to find a crossroad in order to hide the tracks and so they can't hear the change in engines."

Hide the tracks? Change in engines? "What change in engines?"

"When we get to the truck."

What truck? She became alarmed and shivered.

"Are you cold?"

"No," she replied in a tiny voice. He sounded so concerned. He probably had to deliver her intact. To whom? Questions buzzed in her head.

"There it is," he said, "just around this last bend. They did a good job."

She looked quickly and through a slight gap in the trees, she saw a gray truck. It would be impossible to see unless you knew where to look. She pressed her lips together.

Quint could hear that her breathing had quickened. In a gravelly surprise he asked, "Are you scared?"

"No," she replied in a rather high, breathless way.

"You're safe wi' me. You gotta know that."

"Oh, yes. Of course." Her reply was too quick, the words all running together.

"Georgina..." he began, but they had rounded the curve and came to down a travelled east-west road. Quint turned right toward Sacramento—and they were there. A truck stood waiting. It wasn't large and was stopped in the midst of the tracks of other cars, not off to the side of the road. Its motor was running.

As Quint throttled down, the back doors opened and a ramp was extended until it reached full length. Then its outer edge was lowered until it almost touched the ground.

Quint kept the motorcycle's wheels in the truck's tire tracks as they approached, then revved the motor and lifted the front wheel high enough to reach the ramp. He drove the motorcycle up and into the body of the truck next to a car, already there inside, with two men standing beside it.

Georgina was amazed. She looked back. Out there was nothing but snow, an empty road, trees and mountains. One man went cautiously down the ramp and carefully examined the tracks.

Quint got off the machine, and with his attention also focused on the tracks behind, absently helped George to dismount. The other man took charge of the cycle, pushing it onto a rack.

Quint told her to stay back. Then he went to the door and watched carefully. He pointed to one place, and snow from a tub was thrown carefully through a slotted implement so that it didn't splat down in a clump but fell feathered-out. The truck moved forward slowly, and a little snow was judiciously spread where the wheels had rested too long and where the exhaust had discolored the snow.

That fascinated Georgina. This had all been planned and was being very meticulously executed. What on earth did she know that they wanted from her? She had no idea. What if she was to be held for ransom? Who would pay? She considered her hard-nosed, straitlaced, law-abiding father. Would he pay a ransom? She doubted it.

The view of the snow-covered mountain forest and the truck's double tracks, trailing away in the snow, was slowly lost to her as the ramp was pulled back inside and the two big doors were quietly shut and latched. She was locked in there, in total darkness, with three large men.

Then a battery lamp was turned on. The men all looked at her but their examination was only curiosity. She sent sharp glances around and saw there was a pulldown seat on one side of the truck wall.

Quint put out a hand for hers, but not wanting to make it too easy for him, she didn't take it. She was her non-ransom-paying father's daughter.

Quint's quick study weighed her and he said firmly, "You're 'kay. Trust me."

She eyed him cautiously. His language had changed.

"It'll warm up quick," he assured her, taking her gloved, reluctant hands and rubbing them, peering into her face, gauging her mood. Then he spoke more slowly. "You will be all right."

She thought that Quint Finnig was not what he seemed. His speech was again careful. Her body pulled back as he tried to lead her past the car, over to the pulldown seat.

The other men stood swaying to the movement of the truck, silently watching Finnig cope with her. They were probably thinking she was just some stubborn female. Their curiosity was avid.

With great concern, which riveted the men's interest, Finnig told her, "The road's rough. We need to sit down. We can't until you do. We're gentlemen."

That brought disbelieving snorts from the watchers.

Georgina shivered.

"Hey, she's cold!" one of the men exclaimed in a western accent. "We told ya to take care of 'er! Here, honey, put this 'round you." He shook out a blanket, filling the space with dust and making the others cough and protest.

With great patience, Quint took the blanket. "Sit down," he told the men.

They did. But their eyes watched with quick interest and they were very alert.

Quint put the blanket around her shoulders so carefully that the men's necks stretched in order to monitor every single nuance of movement. "I'm sorry we couldn't get your things," Quint told Georgina. "We couldn't risk it."

He sat her down on the ledge and strapped her in, blanket and all. "You're freezing!" He was appalled. "We had to have the back open. It'll warm up in just a few minutes."

Hunched, she nodded. She'd pretend it was an everyday occurrence to ride on a motorcycle that went up into a truck that carried a concealed car and then to have men wipe out all evidence of that having happened. Of course. Such things were ordinary.

With a stern look at the two fascinated men, Quint took off his fur-lined jacket and put it around Georgina. It surrounded her with his heat. Then he sat down by her. Quint gave the two watchers his patient gaze and suggested that they relax.

They shifted and began to have a very silly conversation.

"Lotta snow out there."

"Yeah."

"Purrdy on the trees."

"Yeah."

"That's a great machine, but I'd never thought of using it on the snow like Finnig did."

"Me neither."

"That Finnig can do anything." The two grinned at him, pleased they'd puffed him up before his woman. He sighed. They laughed and things got easier between the men.

But not for Georgina.

Quint's jacket made her feel as if she were in an oven, and she fleetingly considered how it must be for a frozen fillet to be baked. Her surface was scorched, but her nervous core was frozen.

She had thought that without his coat, Finnig would be chilly, but sitting next to her, his body continued to heat her. How could she possibly have this feeling of security?

At the lodge, she'd gotten on the back of a motorcycle and driven out of sight. Now she was in the back of a truck going God only knew where. For all practical purposes, she'd simply disappeared into thin air. How would anyone ever find her? Or have any idea how to look for her?

She sat looking around from the nest of the blanket and Quint's coat, warmed by his closeness. Her silly body began to relax. Gradually she absorbed the conversation between the two men and Finnig.

"What's a Chicago boy doing clear out here?" one man asked Quint.

Looking at Georgina, he replied, "Seeing to my interests."

The two men laughed in a very male way, down in their throats.

That exchange caught her attention. If they didn't
know Finnig, they might not know what a serious
thing they were doing, carrying a woman off this way.
She might manage to enlist their help in getting away.
Westerners were honest men, everybody knew that.
They protected women. She could appeal to them
and . . .

"You get tired of her, you let me know," one said.

"After me, buster," the other claimed.

"I saw her before you," the first protested.

She moved closer to Quint. At least he hadn't made
any overt move. Other than kidnapping her.

Looking toward the back of the truck, she found no
way to ignore the fact that the car stood there, waiting. Why was there a car in this truck? It was parked
facing outward, almost as if—

"Car."

Georgina jerked her head around to gaze at the
front of the truck. There was a communications
hookup with the cab. Wasn't that unusual? Wasn't
this whole operation unusual?

The men became silent. Over the noise of the truck's
motor came the powerful sound of another engine.
There was a blare of a horn and the truck slowed,
moving carefully. The car's motor went on past.

"L.A. plates" was the only comment from the
truck's cab.

It was then that Georgina realized the men had been
expecting pursuit. They had known someone at the
lodge would follow, and had devised this elaborate
scheme to avoid being caught. Who at the lodge would
suspect that she had been taken and be interested or

concerned enough to come after her? Susan? How droll. There was no one. What on earth was this about?

Was it Quintus Finnig who was being pursued? Who was he? Why had he involved her?

"The helmets and vests should protect you if there's shooting," Quint told the two men.

"No problem."

Shooting?

"Georgina, you need to give Dave your ski outer clothes. They're going to ride out and make it seem they are us. Dave's the closest we could find who was about your size. Go behind the car. There's a coverall on the trunk that'll fit you. We need that pink outfit to distract any hunters."

"What's going on?" she asked carefully.

"I had to get you away. Don't worry. I'll take care of you. Dave's built a little different, but he can fit in your suit. Go change. I think they're ahead of us. The road oughta be clear. Hurry."

The second man told Georgina, "Quint figured riding this far in the truck would protect us. He didn't like us being too easy a target."

"Target?"

"We only need to be seen at one truck stop. That's coming up. Then Dave'll take off your clothes and we'll just disappear." He snapped his fingers and laughed.

"Quit talking," Quint ordered. "Hurry, Georgina. Call out as soon as you're in the coveralls."

Thoroughly confused, Georgina went to do as she'd been told. She peeled off Frances's pink ski outfit, down to her thermal underwear, and put on the coveralls, which felt like putting on a sheet of ice. "Okay," she called out.

Dave came around the car and pulled on the pink trousers over his own. Carefully he eased the pink jacket's stretch material over his broader shoulders. He was in high spirits and swished a little, laughing. He was acting as men do when they think they're imitating women.

"Why are you going to pretend to be me?" she asked.

He grinned at her. "For a whole lot of money and an adventure." Then, serious, he added, "To help the friend of a friend."

She frowned. "Who would shoot at you?"

"The enemy." He said that in a delighted, low, dramatic voice.

Georgina thought it was just as the sage Elsie MacLean has always said: men are different.

"But they won't really shoot," Dave added. "Finnig is just being careful for us."

As the truck slowed and the two men readied themselves, Georgina thought again that maybe it wasn't she who was in danger, but Finnig. Then why had he come for her? With that question, her interested body decided he wanted to have her with him in some gangland hideaway for entertainment to pass idle time. Her brain hoo-hawed in disbelief. Outside of watching her come down the stairs with her sisters last November, and dancing all the slow dances with her at the reception, what indication did she have that he might be interested in her . . . in that way? None.

Then why was she here in the back of this truck?

There was undoubtedly a very plausible, dull explanation.

A little keyed up, the two men readied themselves, and as the doors were opened and the ramp extended, Finnig cautioned them. They both nodded seriously. They donned the black helmets, and George was annoyed to see that Dave could indeed pass for a female in the pink outfit and the disguising helmet.

Dave pulled her purse from the cycle's luggage box and handed it to her. Then he and the larger man got on the machine with Dave sitting behind. Through his visor, George could barely see the laughter on Dave's face. The two men went down the ramp, and driving on one of the truck's tire tracks, sped away. A pink arm waved, and then they were gone.

"Come," Quint said to her. "We can't let the truck stand long."

He led her to the car's passenger side and put her into her seat, helping her to buckle in. Then he went to the driver's side and got in. He eased the car out matching other cars' tracks, and tooted the horn twice as the rear wheels left the ramp. Georgina looked back and saw the truck moving as the ramp disappeared inside. The doors closed, but the latch hung free.

"We're heading north to Red Bluff to get a plane there," Quint told her. "We figured both the Sacramento and Reno airports would be covered. They might not think we'd go to Red Bluff."

"That's north and back toward the coast."

"Yes."

"What in the world is going on?" she asked.

"Since we don't want to be seen, we'll avoid Interstate 80 and take the back roads. I can drive a car in snow and ice, but mountains are different. I'll explain everything when we get away. I felt you were in danger because of me. When we get to Chicago, I'll show you the pictures of you that I got in the mail."

"Pictures?"

"Yeah."

"Who sent them?"

"I don't know."

Georgina knew that for Quint, that was a lot of chatter. Then in surprise, she inquired, "We're going to Chicago?"

"Yes."

And she said an amazed, "Oh." It was only then that she noted the car was silver, a color that had once been unique but was now very common.

It was obvious to the fugitives that snow skiers had clout in the area. All those tiny roads were plowed, and the travelers drove a long way.

They were on Highway 89 heading for 70 when the first hitch came to their plans. They stopped for gas at a small station in a tiny town, and walking to the rest room, Georgina heard the station attendant say softly to Quint, "So you're Finnig."

With a casualness that was impressive, Quint asked in his careful voice, "Who is Finnig?"

Georgina stopped and stared. Under the circumstances, her curiosity was understandable. She saw the attendant make a brief motion with his hand but his back was to her so she didn't see exactly. A signal? Quint glanced at the gesture, then smiled. Georgina frowned.

"So?" Finnig asked.

"They're showing pictures of the two of you," the man replied, still speaking softly. "You're lucky you took 89 up and didn't go on to Reno. They have the airport covered in Red Bluff—just as a caution. But they're thick as fleas around Reno."

Quint nodded.

"We have a place you can wait. Here's the key and the directions. It has a green door. It's been closed a long time and it's cold. When we got the signal, we made a fire in the cabin and began to get it warmed on the chance you might come this way. It'll take a day or two."

"I appreciate it," Quint replied, pocketing the key and the slip of paper with the directions.

The man was filling the car's gas tank. Quint looked at Georgina, and he winked and moved his head slightly, indicating that she should go on.

Obediently she turned and left them, going to the rest room. It was clean. She looked into the mirror and her face was as blank as she felt. If she were Tate, she would consider this an adventure, but she was Georgina, and she was unsettled. Should she just go along with whatever this was? Or should she decline? What *was* going on? How did this man know Finnig? Clear out here in this remote place in California? What was the signal? Then she remembered that as they had left the lodge, Quint had raised an arm and waved it in a circle. Was that the signal? He'd said he was waving to a friend. Where had the friend been in that snow? It was very strange.

She went back to the car, all ready to say she'd catch a bus.

Quint took her arm, bending his head closer to hers. "It'll be all right. This is a man in a network I was connected with, and he'll help us."

"Why would he do that?"

Quint knew her conduct from now on hinged on his reply, and he realized he must be truthful. She was judging him. He became very uncomfortable and had trouble admitting, "He...admires me." His face flushed.

Georgina was so charmed by his reluctant admission that she decided to follow his directions.

Following directions, Quint drove the car to an isolated shed. There he removed the license plates and battery, putting them into the box on the snowmobile that was parked there. Then still following directions, they rode the snowmobile on a roundabout path until they came to the cabin with the green door.

Quint stopped the snowmobile, got off and needlessly helped Georgina to dismount as he looked around carefully. He unlocked the door and stood aside for her to enter. He brought the car battery inside and set it on the floor by the door. "I'll put the machine in the shed and bring in some wood." Then he went out.

Georgina was left alone in the room. That's all the cabin was—one room. There were two doors at the back, and she went to see where they led. The first was to a bathroom. To keep the pipes from freezing, there was a lightbulb placed in the wooden enclosure where they came out from the ground.

She cautiously turned on the water in the lavatory, and it worked. That lifted her spirits a bit. Then she went out and unlocked the other door and saw that it led outside. She turned back and viewed the limited space. One room. One whole wall was a bookcase of paperbacks. Along another wall was the kitchen. There was a table and four chairs, a sofa and one bed. That was it. One room—and one bed. She folded her arms under her peaked breasts and waited for Quintus Finnig to step inside.

He came in with a great armload of wood. The woodbox was already filled, so he stacked the new firewood next to the box on the floor.

When he was finished and brushing his hands together, she asked, "Is this some kind of setup?"

"How d'you mean?"

Since he'd never given any real indication of *wanting* to get her off by herself, how was she to ask him if he had brought her there to the mountain cabin for carnal purposes? It was a little embarrassing. Lamely she asked, "Why are we here?"

"I'm sorry 'bout this, Georgina." He seemed incapable of looking right at her. "But for your sake, this is the safest place for us right now. It ought to be just a couple of days."

She gasped her indignation in order to cover her shocking flood of sensual joy. "A couple of days?"

"Then we can fly out to Chicago until this thing gets settled."

"Specifically, what 'thing' would that be?"

"Before we get into that, do you know anything about wood fires?" He looked at her. "All Murray said was not to build it too high or we'd get a fire in the chimney wall."

"Who are the people who are looking for us?"

"I don't know."

"Quint, who are you?"

"I'm only a man." There was a long silence. Then he said gently, "About the fire."

"It could use about four logs. I'll do it."

"Show me how."

"You weren't a Boy Scout?"

"Hardly."

Hardly? Why... hardly? What had he been doing at age twelve? She knelt down in front of the fireplace and stirred the coals, shaking down the ashes before laying some of the larger logs across the smaller ones.

He watched her. "That's all?"

"Yep. Unless the fire dies out. Then it's a little more complicated.

"I always thought fireplaces were in the middle of the wall."

"Being in the corner this way, there are no cold corners. See? The warmth goes across the whole room."

"Georgina, I'm sorry about this. There was nothing else to do but get you away. I couldn't risk you getting held."

"Who would want to hold me, and for what reason?"

Hold her? Quint's soul groaned to hold her. "When I came to see you in December, somebody saw me go to your place. I got pictures in the mail—pictures of you at the grocery, driving your car, coming out of your apartment. No message, no threat, just the pictures. But I don't take chances. I had to get you away. I had it arranged, and you . . . complicated it by going skiing. We had to form a . . . contingency plan. I didn't know what might happen to you at the lodge. It was dangerous for you to be there. Whoever sent those pictures could have been there, too. Somebody was. We were followed. They're hunting us. I'm sorry. But I'll take care of you. I promise you'll be okay. Don't be afraid."

There was another silence. She was amazed he could speak at that length and then what he'd said was simply unreal. Someone had taken pictures of her? And she hadn't known it! That made her shiver. How dared anyone invade her privacy by taking pictures of her without her permission? "You have no idea who these people are?"

"No. And if we're careful, we won't find out."

So here she was, in a one-room cabin in the mountains with the smoky, shadowy Quintus Finnig, who was, at the very best, unsuitable. At the very worst, he was a man who drove her senses crazy. And she was supposed to stay in this room, which had one bed, for a couple of days with this man? How was she supposed to control herself?

Quint waited for some signal that she was okay. He ached to comfort her. But if he allowed himself to touch her, what would happen? He might lose his tightly held control. He'd tried to deny himself the pleasure of looking at her. When that became impossible, he'd thought he might look and not touch, but that wasn't how it worked. He'd probably have to take snow baths and sleep in the shed.

She took a breath, and he couldn't prevent himself from looking at her there in the firelight in that much-too-intimate cabin.

She said, "My family is going to get sick and tired of having a daughter missing. First Tate and now me."

"No one knows you're missing."

"I'm . . . not sure that's good."

"Georgina, you don't have to be scared of *me* because I'm keeping you safe."

She laughed softly. "How can I tell?"

He knew by her look that she meant to be funny, but he groaned as if in pain. He wondered for which particular sin that he'd committed was he roasting in the hell of sharing this cabin with Georgina—and trying not to touch her.

Five

To distract himself from Georgina, Quint moved restlessly over to the counter that served as the kitchen section of their single room and began emptying the grocery sacks there. "Looks like they stocked us for the winter." Then he could have bitten his tongue—his words might make her feel trapped there with him indefinitely. She was spooked enough as it was.

He made his voice a droning, soothing repetition: "Pancake batter, pasta, dried milk, cocoa, coffee, canned ham, eggs. They did a good job of it. Are you hungry? It's dark already. It gets that way early this time of the year." He was acutely aware of her silence. He wondered if the time could come when he could really talk to her. Or should he avoid the temptation for that intimacy? Would it only tear him apart to know her well enough to share ideas, to exchange opinions, to experience the openness of knowing each other's thoughts?

He concentrated on the food supply. "There's wine." He pulled out a bottle and looked at the label. "Why not sit by the fire and have a small glass to warm yourself?"

"No, thank you."

"Sit down, Georgina. We're going to be here for a while."

Georgina gave him a quick glance. If he was any other man, being there would be no problem for her emotions.

But he thought she was panicking. Making his voice very calm, he told her, "I'm no threat to you, Georgina. I promise."

Well, damn. She'd been on her own for almost ten years, and she'd never had any real problem with any man. She'd never allowed a situation to develop that could be dangerous to a woman. Nor had she ever gone to or been caught in an isolated place with any man. Now, here she was in the classic situation—a cabin in the woods, with a man who had intrigued her from first sight, one room, one bed, night was coming on—and he promised he was no threat to her.

With this man the isolation was different. He was the hero type. There could be no outside danger. He had cleverly avoided whatever confrontation that might have happened.

They were going to be together there for a while. There was snow outside, and it was cold; but inside it was warm and—she almost smiled—quite intimate.

She glanced around the cozy room, with its unmatched furniture and shelves of worn paperback books.

She paced the limited floor space, covered by an old braided rug, and she drew in a patient breath. It would be up to her. He apparently was a bit interested in her, or he wouldn't have come to Sacramento for that strange, nothing visit. And he was concerned about her. Even if he wasn't seriously interested, when he'd found that danger might threaten her, he'd come for her, organized a rescue. And . . . here they were.

Obviously, the seduction was up to her. This might be the only time she could know what it might be like to make love with such a man. No other man had ever tempted her to taste this particular side of living. Quint did, whoever or whatever he was. And his ambivalence probably contributed to her being intrigued.

So this was her opportunity. Here. Would he brush her off? Would he be shocked? Would he huff and be scandalized? Was he involved with another woman? Such a man wouldn't be long alone. What would he do if she approached him? She turned to look back at him.

. . . and she caught him watching her with the most . . . vulnerable expression. She smiled. It might not be so difficult, after all.

With a little flair, she strolled the few steps over to the kitchen area . . . and Quint. "A little wine might be just the thing. How nice of them to have included some."

"I hadn't known the network still worked." That was out before he could stop it. It had surprised him when he'd been able to reach the first contact and he was bowled over by the spreading response and the cooperation.

"What sort of network?" she inquired encouragingly.

He hesitated, then said shortly, "Fund-raising," having said that much, he stopped dead, turning his attention to pouring the wine.

"Charity?" Rather drolly, she probed.

"Yeah." He handed her a glass of wine. "Here. Sip it. Go over by the fire. You'll be warm there."

"Let's pull the sofa over in front of it and sit on that."

"I'm too hot to sit that close." Quint gave her a quick look, and saw that her face was bland. She probably would believe he meant close to the fire, but he didn't dare sit beside her—he'd scorch her. "We ought to leave the sofa there for now. Just until the room gets warmer. The sofa would block the heat." That would be true.

Concentrating on how to act seductively, Georgina bit into the side of her lower lip.

His glance went to her mouth, and he moved restlessly. "I'd better go out and see if everything's okay."

Disappointed, she watched forlornly as he left the cabin. What was his problem? Maybe he was shy. She bubbled with laughter. Him? Shy? No way. But maybe he was—with her. She wondered if Bill and Angus had warned him away from her? Was that the problem? Had they told *him* he was unsuitable? Had they dared to do that to such a man? They'd certainly made no bones about telling her.

But at thirty-one, she could make up her own mind as to who was suitable and who was not. Besides, all she wanted was a flirtation. But what if he was married?

She looked at her watch and saw it was suppertime. She finished putting the groceries away, and with Quint's pre-Christmas demolition of her whole chicken in mind, she made a hearty supper. Vegetable soup, pasta, someone's still-wrapped, leftover Christmas fruitcake and the wine. She checked to be sure there was a goodly supply—there was—and she smiled. It was nice to have ample stock. Her seduction plan could take a day or so.

So when he came back inside with another load of wood, without turning toward him, Georgina mentioned, "We don't have a phone, if you need to call...your wife." Then she looked at him.

He'd been stacking the new logs on top of the first load he'd brought inside, but he paused to look up at her. "I don't have a wife. I never got married,"

"Neither have I." Why was she breathless?

The fact she'd asked the Woman's Question sent a tingling lick of excitement down him. Why had she asked? He tried to breathe normally. That was stupid; he hadn't breathed normally since he'd first met her and his whole system had gone off kilter, just seeing one particular woman. Just thinking about her wrecked him. It didn't make sense. And being around her made everything worse. Better. Hell.

But he ought not to fool himself. She was the kind of woman who would worry about other people worrying. It had been compassion that had made her ask about a wife. Georgina was a lady, and like Mrs. Adams at Field's had said, a lady is courteous, considerate and compassionate. Georgina hadn't meant anything personal, asking that.

"Are you a good cook?" Georgina queried him in a friendly way. "Do you have any...health problems?" She held her breath, waiting for his answer.

He stood slowly. "I'm clean."

She was startled by his word choice. It was what she wanted to know but, well, she didn't want it stated quite so blatantly. So she hurried on with another question. "No diet? You can eat anything?"

Quint shifted and looked around a little awkwardly. "No diet," he mumbled. Hell, he'd thought his dreams had come true there for that minute. What a fool he was. He'd have to watch his damned tongue.

So he was silent. Just the way he'd been as he'd consumed her entire chicken in Sacramento. Georgina was disappointed. She did try. She talked about football, bragging about the 49ers and casting subtle criticism on the Chicago Bears. He grunted in absent-minded agreement. So she tried politics.

He said, "They're all crooks." That finished that.

What about Ireland? He just shook his head. The Middle East? He shrugged.

She said his name slowly, "Quintus Finnig. Are you Irish?"

"Probably."

"Don't you know?"

Quint lifted his head and looked at her fully. "I was a street kid, long ago when there wasn't none. Any that anybody noticed, but there's always been kids living that way." He dismissed the subject and went back to eating.

"How did you live?"

"Not very easy." For the first time in his life he was ashamed. He wanted to be a magic man for her, the right man, but he was nothing. "Unsuitable," Angus had said. Angus was right. She deserved more than just Quint Finnig. He looked at his plate, his face still, his eyes bitter.

Her voice was soft. "That must have been tough. What happened in the winters?"

"I made it."

"Obviously." Her word was soft.

He was silent.

Georgina knew he didn't want to talk, but she'd been encouraged by his several sentences, which must have been unusual. "A hundred years ago, one of my ancestors was a street child. In the East there was this organization that encouraged western farmers to take in street kids. The organization checked out the families to be sure the kids wouldn't be abused or overworked, and monitored the program. A man in Texas took four boys, including my ancestor. They all turned out well. They were the lucky ones. I wish someone had helped you. It must have been very hard for you."

Quint had never had any sympathy before, and it shocked him that it touched him in that bleak place inside him that he'd always ignored. He continued eating carefully, as he'd been instructed not long ago, but he glanced at her and said in a growl, "It was no big deal."

She smiled at his sober face. "An iron man?"

"Yeah."

"We played street games when I was a child."

Street games? He thought she could have no idea what real street games were. "You did?"

"Red rover, kick the can—"

"Red rover? What was that?"

"A game to get to the other side of the street."

That was what he needed—a way to cross to her side of the street. He was on the wrong side. How could he ever cross over?

Encouraging him to keep talking to her, George asked, "Did you play those same ones?"

"No."

Inevitably, the time came to sleep. Quint took the blankets off the bed and held them before the fire to warm them.

"I'll sleep on the sofa," Georgina said firmly.

"No."

"I don't intend to have to arm wrestle you over this sofa. I prefer it. It's closer to the fireplace, so I'll be cozy and warm. If you think the bed is better, you sleep there and freeze. I want the sofa. I have first dibs on it. I said it first." She gave him a cool, competitive look.

He smiled a little. "Okay."

She pretended disgust. "You preferred the bed all along, right?"

"I'm bigger'n you."

"I'll be warm," she sassed.

He didn't reply. He was thinking of how he could singe her wings and toast her to a turn. He could . . .

But he couldn't think like that. He'd better go outside and cool off.

He picked up a sack by the door and gave it to her. "They collected some things for you. We couldn't get your clothes from the lodge without risking a guy getting caught. We didn't want to take the chance. I don't know what's in that bag, but that's what they got for you. I'll be outside for a while, looking around. Good night."

"Good night, Quint. Thank you."

"I'm sorry I got you into this. I wasn't thinking." He opened the door and went out, closing it behind him.

Georgina looked at the lumpy sofa with distaste. But she couldn't allow a man the size of Quint to struggle to sleep on that. She'd do well enough. She'd rather be in bed with him. Next to him, to his heat. Under him. The single subject of his attention. Ah, well, she still had tomorrow.

Poor little Quintus Finnig, a street child. How had that happened?

She dumped the contents of the sack out onto the bed and chuckled. Along with a toothbrush was a sheer nightgown. That nightgown in this cold cabin? She shook her head. There were also underwear, a couple of T-shirts and two flannel shirts. All were too large. But the suppliers had tried.

She took one of the quilts and draped it over a chair, which she pushed close to the fireplace. After brushing her teeth, she put on one of the oversize T-shirts and a pair of the droopy panties. She rinsed out her own things and hung them by the fire.

She transferred one of the pillows from the bed to the sofa, wrapped the warmed blanket around her and curled on the sofa. She was tired enough and dozed almost instantly. Vaguely she heard Quint come back inside.

The next thing she knew, he had gently scooped her up. She lay in his arms as he stood silently still. She longed to peek at him, but knowing she was supposed to be asleep, she lay lax and kept her eyes closed. As if in sleep, she curled her face against his throat and sighed. She felt him tremble. Maybe it wouldn't be so difficult, after all.

Very carefully Quint lowered his head, put his face against her hair and breathed in her scent. Every fiber in him was alert and rigid. His muscles shivered. With only the very tops of his lungs he was breathing in small, smothering sips of air. He lifted his face and took a deep, silent breath through his mouth. Then he carried her over and lay her in the bed, covering her with warmed blankets.

Georgina realized almost immediately that he'd first gotten into the bed and warmed it with his body heat. As she snuggled down, she knew she'd never felt anything so erotic in all her life. He stood beside the bed for a long time, and gradually, she went back to sleep, knowing he hadn't lied, that he really meant to take care of her. Whatever was happening, she could trust him. He was an honorable man. How could he be unsuitable?

It had to be a long time later when he again came to the bed. She was electrified. She lay silent and still as he lifted back the blankets. He'd come to her? She waited for him to get in beside her. The inside of her stomach shivered in excitement and her breasts became sensitive and full as her core heated.

Carefully his hands slid under her and he lifted her and held her for a tense minute. Then he quietly carried her over and laid her on the sofa, wrapping the blanket around her. He stood looking down at her before he moved away.

Now what was that all about? Just what was he doing, moving her around when she was asleep? He'd found out he couldn't sleep on that lumpy sofa so he'd put her back? And since she'd pretended to sleep through both moves, how was she going to tweak him about this? Well, rats!

She lay there, disgusted. Listening, thinking, plotting. Then she heard a soft snore. He was asleep! How could he go to sleep when she was in such a turmoil? She peeked at her watch. It was almost six o'clock. She'd slept all night in his bed. He was manipulating her, letting her think she'd had her own way, when he'd spent the night on this miserable sofa. Now, what was she going to do about that? She fretted for a while, but the day before had been unsettling, to say the least, so she went back to sleep. Her last thought was that Quintus Finnig was a crafty man who had his way. And how could she get him to want his wily way with her?

The next morning Quint inquired how the sofa had been for sleeping. And there was a definite smug look in his slight smile. It was impossible for Georgina to grin back, because she wasn't supposed to know he'd tricked her. So she said, "I'm glad I got dibs on the sofa. It was very restful and comfortable. How was your bed?"

Quint looked down at the oatmeal in his bowl. "Fine," he answered smoothly. But his body shivered with desire as he remembered getting back into the bed and feeling the heat left by her body and smelling her fragrance on his pillow. He'd had to pretend to snore so that, on the sofa, she could get back to sleep. He allowed her to believe that she'd fooled him.

They explored their prison. Along with one pair of old wooden skis, they found a sled in the shed loft and tried it on a gentle slope close by. Near that gentle slope there was a slope with an awesome dropoff, but they shunned it. The sled was big enough for two, and they had a good, lighthearted time.

The air was still, crisp and pure. It was like breathing wine. She doubted he'd ever been on a sled before, and she assumed the lead at first.

He'd "sledded" on pieces of cardboard. Even street children play.

And it was he who began the snowman. She said he was sexist, and made a snow woman, calling her Mary Anne. He said the snowman was Jiggs.

"Jiggs? I've never known anyone named Jiggs. What made you think of that name?"

"I knew a kid by that name. He was named after a comic-strip character. He was little and his hair stuck out. He had big eyes and a pug nose. He was a good guy."

"You say 'was.' What happened to him?"

"He was knifed."

She looked at him in shock.

If nothing else had made it clear to him, Quint knew then how far apart they were. Knifings weren't shocking to him. To her, they were. Their lives were far apart. There was no magic of a red-rover game that could get him across to her side of the street.

They had ham-and-cheese sandwiches for lunch. She had one, he had three. There were also pickles, potato chips and hot chocolate.

It began to snow again. The same winter rains of the lower, warmer levels of Sacramento made the slopes deep with snow in the mountains.

The two in the cabin went through the wall of paperback books, commenting, comparing and pretending they were looking for something to read. Whoever had selected them had chosen with good taste. Georgina was surprised by the number of books Quint *had* read—and that she hadn't. He didn't look like a reader. What *did* a reader look like?

With a book in her hands, she curled at one end of the sofa, contented. Well, not quite. There was still a restless agitation buried deep in her that had no ready cure. But Quint was there in the room with her, and just that gave her pleasure.

She had expected him to sit beside her, but he didn't. He sat on the floor and leaned back against the sofa. For Georgina, that was almost better. She could pretend to read, but leave her eyes resting on him.

She thought his head was beautifully shaped, and her fingers longed to play with his thick hair. He had nice ears—not small and stingy or great, flapping ones. Those shells were just right, and her tongue sought along the inside of her mouth, wanting to explore the ridges and valleys of those shells. And his eyelashes. Ah, such thick eyelashes, and on a man.

Quint knew that she was looking at him—she wasn't turning pages as he did. How long could he pretend to read when he knew he had her attention? How long could he control his body's response to her watching him? My God, he thought, could she be interested in him? Or was she only curious?

He'd take any kind of reaction that he could get from her. Anything but indifference. He'd even settle for just her curiosity. How many men had lost themselves in her? How many men had she had? She looked so innocent. Her reactions were so uncalculated. How many men had wanted her? And what had happened to them? Had they all died of love? He might.

She'd been awake in his arms last night—both times that he'd carried her. She'd known he held her and she'd given no sign. She'd put her face against his neck and turned him to stone with his desire. He hadn't been able to move. And she'd been as still as a mouse. That was all that had saved her. If she'd moved or spoken to him, she'd have spent the rest of the night with him, against him, close... He'd better go outside and do something.

He rose, keeping his back to her, and stretched, pretending to yawn. "If I'm going to stay awake, I'd better get outside. I'm not used to this lazy life." He put his hands into his pockets and walked the few steps over to the fireplace to check the blaze. He removed the fire screen, added another log to be sure it kept going, then replaced the screen.

Georgina wondered why he didn't suggest they both get into his bed and nap together. She rose, too, and stretched. "I'll go with you," she said. If she napped she'd toss and turn all night long. She needed to be dead tired.

They went back to the shed and discussed whether the single pair of skis they'd seen were big enough for him to try. She convinced him.

He asked, "You're sure I won't break my neck?"

"Trust me."

He frowned. "Isn't that what the snake told Eve?"

She laughed.

It sounded marvelous to Quint. It was the first time he'd ever teased a woman. He found the brief success filled him with a sense of power. He'd tease her into his bed. "You look like a woman who'd..." What word could he use? A word that wouldn't offend her. He couldn't use *trick* or *fool* or *lie*. What word?

"What do I look like I'd do?"

And in perfect honesty, he said, "Drive a man crazy."

Saucily, she pretended to consider that as she looked off into the distance. Then she shook her head and turned her gaze back to him. "No. I prefer my men uncrazy."

"Around you?" he exclaimed in real disbelief.

It had been the perfect thing to say. Georgina laughed, flattered. She thought how impatient she'd always been with flattery, but Quint's words had pleased her.

He surprised himself when he then said, "You're beautiful, Georgina."

Pleased, she denied it. "It's the day. It's so gorgeous that everything in it is pretty. Look at those scrawny old trees, those black branches against the snow. Breathtaking."

He said "Yes." But he wasn't looking at the trees.

With the ski boots jammed on his feet and locked onto the skis, she showed him the rudiments of walking and herringboning up a slope or sidestepping up a hill. Then snowplowing to stop, and—in order to turn around—how to swing a ski up and over and down, then to lift the other around into place, parallel. He got tangled with that one, fell with calculation, and allowed her to untangle him. She laughed and had a marvelous time. He watched her.

She insisted he try the edge of their sledding slope. He was doubtful. "My God, do you expect me to go clear down there?"

She nodded. "It's like flying."

"It's like suicide."

She thought that was funny. "Go on!"

"If I break my leg, get the sled."

She sobered. "Try the slope tomorrow."

"Today."

"No! I don't want you hurt."

The thrill he felt at her words carried him all the way to the bottom of the slope. It felt like he was flying. His snowplow didn't work and he made a strange, banking curve that barely missed a tree. Her scream

was music to his ears, so he contrived a plausible
tumble.

She blundered all the way down through the deep
snow, floundering to his side. "Are you all right?"
She flung herself down and leaned over him.

He pulled her on top of him and kissed her, making her gasp and widening her eyes. They were both
very serious as they stared at each other. Then he
grinned slowly. "A piece of cake."

Georgina shook herself out of her trance and accused with no heat at all, "You've been sand skiing for
twenty years along the Indiana Dunes. Right?"

"Nope. My instructor was Georgina Lambert."

"Can you get back up to the top of the slope?"

"My feet are dead. The boots are too tight. I'll
walk."

They took the path they'd trod that morning when
they'd sledded, and they stomped back into the cabin,
leaving melting snow clear over to the fireplace. Re-
moving the strange boots, he said, "You need to sweep
it out or we'll have puddles."

While his feet thawed, he lounged on the floor by
the fire, and she got to fuss over him. She found some
dry socks and eased them onto his feet. He watched
her with yellow flames in his brown eyes as she worked
at the socks.

She put another log on the fire and sat back on her
heels. He smiled at her. But she could only stare.
Gradually he sobered. He became quicker in his
movements, his breath, his eyes, as she became more
languid. He slowly reached out a hand, and she laid

hers on his. His was so much bigger. *He* was bigger. He tugged her to him, and she didn't resist. That surprised him and affected him very much.

As she was drawn closer, she put her other hand on his chest and felt his heart thundering along. Her lips parted and she could feel the reactions to his closeness flickering through her body in an amazing way.

He put her other hand on his chest and moved his hands to her body to pull her to him as he lifted his mouth to capture her lips. She moved her own head to allow their mouths to meet perfectly. And they kissed.

As light dances on broken water, so the thrills shimmered through Georgina's body. Quint trembled and his breathing became harsh. He pulled her over him, her body dragging up his, and his arms closed around her as he kissed her a second, much more serious time.

Time was distorted as they clung to each other, their mouths eager and greedy. Their bodies were tightly pressed together, her breasts loving the pressure of being against his hard chest. She wanted more.

She had begun to moan when he heard the high whine of a snowmobile coming close. She didn't even hear it. He snapped his head up in disbelief. Then he put her aside. "Company? Get your jacket and boots on. Hurry!"

She looked around in a sexual daze, unseeing.

"Hurry, honey. We want to be outside."

She frowned, wondering why in hell they wanted to be outside now.

"Georgina, I don't know who's coming. Let's get out of here."

Only then did she hear the approaching machine.

Six

There wasn't just one snowmobile, there were several. Who?

Quint and Georgina went out the back door. In a raking glance, he surveyed the snowy landscape and told her, "This way."

They went to the top of the sharp drop that would take an expert skier to negotiate. Quint instructed quickly as he pointed along the wind-scoured edge where the snow was not so deep. "If you have to run, go that way. See? Then go around this hill to the track, bear left and go straight. You will come to the town. Go to the service station and find Murray. Do you understand?"

"Where will you be?"

"I may have to stay here awhile."

She wondered what he meant by that.

He meant to prevent anyone from following her. He cautioned, "Be quiet."

"Heads up!" a voice called suddenly, and a group of five skiers swooped down, surprising the pair. They stopped nearby. Their spokesman said, "We're patrol. Are those your friends coming? They aren't locals."

"Do me a favor," Quint urged. "Say this is your place."

"Intruders?" another man asked.

"Very." Quint grinned like a wolf.

"Got it," the first man said. A couple of the others nodded, their attention turned back toward the sound of the approaching snowmobiles.

Quint tugged at George's arm. "Let's get out of sight."

They moved away carefully, their dark clothing blending with the tree limbs and underbrush. The falling snow covered them slowly, catching on the flat planes of their heads and bodies, blurring their outlines.

Quint pulled up his black turtleneck and tugged down his black knitted cap until only a slit remained so that he could watch. Sound carried in the stillness—they could hear readily.

The skiers waited, strung out unevenly by the track. Their manner of spreading out would make them rather hard to surprise or control. Georgina wondered who they were, and from where had they come? Patrol? It was probably that exactly.

As the machines approached, one of the skiers lifted a pole to stop them. "Ho, there!"

The snowmobiler slowed and came closer. Above the sound of the motors idling, the first skier called, "This is private property. No trespassing. Sorry. This whole mountain is off-limits to snowmobiles."

"There's a trail," commented a man with a smooth voice.

"Strictly for locals to get to their cabins."

"Whose place is this one?"

As he'd promised Quint, the skier claimed it. "Mine."

"Your name?"

"Why?"

"We're looking for a man."

"Who?" the skier asked.

But the man avoided replying. Instead he asked, "Any strangers around?"

"Go to one of the filling stations in town. They keep track of who's around."

There was a long hesitation and glances were exchanged among the riders. Then they turned the machines and went away.

The skiers watched them go. When the snowmobiles were out of sight, Quint left their shelter and walked over to the skiers. "Thanks."

The man viewed him coolly. "Who were they?"

"I don't know. It's possible that they've been following us."

"Who sent you out here?"

"Tom Murray."

"I'll check with him."

Quint nodded once. "He'll back me."

"We'll be around. Keep your nose clean."

"Pure," Quint responded softly.

The skiers gave Georgina a lingering glance and smiled for the first time. "Take care of her."

"I'm doing my damnedest," Quint replied.

The skiers grinned widely then and one said, "That's understandable."

The patrol split. Some went through the trees while others effortlessly jumped off over the sharp drop, and Georgina sucked in her breath for them. When they could no longer be seen in the falling snow, she said, "They've gone down that awesome slope. Vanished."

"I'd bet they aren't far."

Georgina turned big eyes to Quint. "Who were the men on the snowmobiles?"

"I honestly don't know. We may have to move."

She looked around. "It seemed so safe here."

"I'll take care of you," he promised yet again.

Silently, Quint wondered if the men would come back. The skiers would tell Murray, and he would get word back to Quint if they ought to move. For now it was best that they stay put. What a lucky thing, for the patrol to turn up at just that time. Who were they? The local police? Quint smiled, really amused.

He put his arm around Georgina's shoulders to turn her back toward the cabin.

"This is all very strange," she said.

"I got people working on the pictures. The paper they're printed on can be traced."

"Why would anyone take pictures of me?" she asked impatiently.

"To make me sweat." He meant to make him worry.

"Pictures of me make you sweat?" She scoffed at the idea.

He grinned at her and took her into his arms, holding her close to him. Against the side of her head, he said in a low and growly voice, "You make me sweat in more ways than you'd ever guess." Then he kissed her in a remarkable way as she stood there against him in the snow.

With her feet and hands frozen, with her feeling scared and chilled, he set her pit on fire. It felt very strange. Then he picked her up and carried her inside through the back entrance, set her on her feet, locked and bolted the door. Then he went around closing the window shutters and barring them.

His taking all those precautions made her shiver.

He went to the bookcase and examined it carefully. He reached up and flipped a latch on the top of one section; then he squatted down, fumbled around for another, and flipped it. After that, he just stood up, gave her a grin, and pulled the section out and swung it aside. There were stairs leading down.

"What on earth?" she exclaimed.

"It's a strange world. People do as they must. It could be an escape from hungry spring bears coming inside, or snow-blocked doors. Having this solves several things. We can stay for a while. Come on; let me show you how this works."

After all the years of living with her sister Tate and Tate's imagination, here was a real hidden wall and secret staircase. "Shades of Nancy Drew," she murmured. Cautiously, she followed him down into a small room that had been chiseled out of the mountain rock.

"Nancy Drew?" He wasn't paying real attention. He picked up a flashlight and shone it around. Its beam was bright enough to signal a plane.

She wasn't too surprised that he didn't know about Nancy Drew. At least she'd found something he hadn't yet read. "How did you know this was here?"

"Murray wouldn't put us in a trap. There had to be a way out." He found a bench that swung aside, leaving a crawl space. He squatted down and shone the light into the tunnel. "It goes to the shed or past it to the slope."

"Oh." After some thought, she asked, "What does Tom Murray do for a living?"

Quint stood and looked amazed that she'd ask. Speaking in that peculiarly slow way of his that made it seem as if he was carefully choosing his words, he replied, "He runs a filling station in town." He turned off the light, set the flashlight down and almost went up the stairs ahead of her. But then he stepped aside and waited.

As she passed him, she asked, "Why did the skiers send the snowmobilers into town to the filling stations?"

Following her up the short flight, he replied, "Everyone around here has to buy gas for something or the other. The station attendants know everybody." He swung the bookcase back into place and carefully latched it. "This'll let them know there're snowmobilers riding around where they're not supposed to be, and that they're strangers looking for somebody. In town, they could give a name and we'll know if it's my name. Sending them into town allowed the skiers to avoid a confrontation."

"Smart."

He took her face between his big, hard hands. "Georgina," he whispered, then asked seriously, "what are you doing to me?"

That made her a little indignant. "What am I doing to you! How like a man to get a woman into this situation and then blame her!"

"We're here alone. You have to know how bad I want you. I don't know what to do."

How could such a man be helpless? She looked up at him, questioningly.

"I don't have any protection for you."

She felt her face heat as she corrected, "There's a box of condoms in the linen closet."

He went to check and came back grinning. He turned out both hands awkwardly as he said, "Uh, we were interrupted."

She was freezing from being outside in the cold but she shivered mostly from nerves. With the intrusion of strangers only barely past, she was surprised that he could expect to take up exactly where he'd left off. Curious, she inquired, "Do you feel so secure that you can now be distracted?"

Slowly and in a deep voice, he asked in turn: "So you know you distract me?"

"I wasn't the one who could hear the motors."

He laughed such a throaty, delicious laugh as he took her against him. "Kiss me, woman. I'm starving for you."

She wondered why the devil he hadn't been this way in Sacramento? She allowed him to hold her body close but she put her forearms on his chest and tilted her face up to his. "Why didn't you give me some indication that you liked me in Sacramento?"

"I was there," he replied simply, with totally male logic.

"Yes." She could agree he had been there. "But you didn't talk to me, or touch me, or do anything at all."

His breathing roughened, his face became serious, his eyes grew intent. "Did you want me to touch you? How? Tell me what you want."

"I don't know," she whispered. "Wing it," she whispered.

He groaned in agony, crushing her to him. "Wing it? You drive me crazy. I am sick with love for you. Ask how sick, and I'll tell you I asked Mrs. Adams at Field's to recommend some *poetry*. I've read the love poems from all time since I met you. The words I've got are crude. I read their words and hate them because I didn't think of them for you."

She was so touched that tears came. "Oh, Quint, I didn't think you could even see me."

"Every time I close my eyes, I see you. You're every blonde head on the street, and I'm sunk when she's not you."

"I gave you up."

He shook his head. "No, you didn't."

"I tried."

"Me, too." With great restraint, he kissed her gently in sips.

His control slipping, he kissed her more quickly. Then, breathing deeply, his arms tightening around her, he kissed her hungrily.

That he wanted her affected her so that she began to weep. And his arms, hands and kisses turned gentle again. But he trembled, his hands shook and he began to sweat. His body was so hot to her cold one.

She burrowed against him and made his head reel, but he slowly released himself from her grasping hands. She stood where he'd abandoned her. She looked abandoned. He ripped off his black jacket, watching her, then turned hurriedly to lean down and put two logs on the fire. Then he rose and came back to her.

Hugging her closely, he groaned with the feel of her in his arms and against him. It was as if he'd never hugged a woman before, and he knew that was true. He loved Georgina.

But he knew there was no possible way that he could take her to Chicago and live there with her, happily ever after. They were from different sides of the street. He was unsuitable. He couldn't fit into her world, and God knew she could never be happy in his. His groan then was one of anguish.

He knew that he should leave her alone. He'd be lost if he ever tasted her. He should let her go. He'd been right all along not to touch her. He commanded his arms to let go of her. They wouldn't. He stiffened and tried to make his body step back, but his feet refused to move. He attempted to ease her away from him, but instead, his hands tightened possessively around her. His voice was roughened. "Georgina, we're no good for each other.

She tilted her head back and looked into his eyes. So he kissed her. Against his will and all good reason, he kissed her yet again. One big hand went to cup the back of her head.

He was hooked. He lifted his mouth from hers as he released a shuddering breath. He would not give her up. He would try to fit into her world. Mrs. Adams would help him. He could do it.

All of his determination was in his next kiss. Finally he lifted his mouth and stared at her, memorizing her.

She managed to say, "Don't kiss me that way unless you mean it."

"Georgina," he murmured passionately. And he went right ahead and kissed her again.

The soft chuckle in her throat set his hair on end and made all his muscles rigid and even affected the very essence of his being. He'd never in his thirty-eight years experienced anything so profound. He ended the kiss, his reaction to her scaring him a little. He was giving control of himself to her.

Georgina saw that his serious regard was then different from any way he'd ever looked at her. She was aware of its meaning—he was committed to her. It was an all-the-way, until-death commitment. That rather shocked her, but she simultaneously realized she felt the same way. Nothing else mattered but that they stay together, past any obstacle.

He picked her up as he had the night before, but this time it was just to hold her. It was a very primitive reaction of a man claiming a woman for his own. He had chosen her. It was a decision between them more binding than a marriage ceremony, and they both understood that.

Breathing shakily, he kissed her again. Their mouths melded, and he felt as if he'd just stepped into fire. He was burning with need of her.

Holding her, he allowed her to slide down him in an exquisite torture, until she stood on her own feet. Then he undressed her carefully while he ripped off his own clothes.

They stood naked before each other. She saw that his breathing was labored, his face almost stark as he looked at her. "Georgina," he said softly. Then he stepped forward and held her cool body to his scorching one, and his kiss was gentle again. His trembling hands barely pressed against her back. It was as if he thought she'd break.

She was so slender, so fragile. Her nipples were pink and taut. Her body's decoration echoed the blonde of her hair, and she was so beautiful that he was a little afraid of her.

She smiled up at him and reached her fingers to his dark hair. She relaxed against him and ran her hands along his rigid shoulders in a pleasure of touching, and she rubbed her breasts against his textured chest. She almost drove him mad, making him shudder.

It was she who led him to the bed. She lifted the blankets and crawled in, and he was a helpless observer. She lay down and patted the bed next to her, amused that she was encouraging her own seduction. She was touched that he was hesitant, charmed by him.

Then she frowned and gasped. The bed was icy! She sat up and flung back the covers.

"What's wrong?" he demanded.

"This bed is *cold*. I'd rather be on the rug."

He couldn't allow that. "No. I'll fix it." He got into bed and pulled her over on top of his burning body, then drew the blankets up over them both.

She laughed and said, "I've found the answer to electric blankets. You!" She snuggled and moved, and he groaned. Instantly she stilled. "Am I too heavy?"

"No. I want you."

"I did suspect that."

His rigid hands moved down her bare back in exquisite pleasure. "Georgina..." He seemed to need to say something more, but after speaking her name, he forgot what it was. He closed his eyes against the tide of his longing.

"I've never done this before," she confessed. "I don't know what to do next. I feel awkward—" she laughed softly "—but willing to learn."

His hands paused. "You're a...virgin?"

"That's a logical assumption." She was a little defensive. "If I've never tried it before, I must be, right?"

He frowned. "I've heard it hurts the first time. I don't want to hurt you."

There was a short silence, then she made a move, as if to get off his hard, trembly body. His arms clamped her to him, and he said earnestly, "I'll be careful."

She smiled a little and relaxed back on him. She kissed his chin, his mouth, his chest, and then looked at him. He was very serious. "Please?" she asked.

Moving first his shoulders, then his hips, he maneuvered them into the middle of the bed, then he turned and laid her in the nest left by his heat. He raised up on his elbow and lay his hot hand on her stomach. "I love you, Georgina."

She reached up and pulled his head down to hers. Given a choice, he might only have explored her, touching, tracing, kissing, suckling, getting her used to him. But with her bold move, he couldn't *not* make love with her. His need was beyond denial. And she wanted him.

Even then, had she been hesitant or fearful, he might have controlled himself; but she set out to entice when he was already lost to her. She was fascinating to him. She made sounds that sent shivers up his skin and down the length of him. She made him gasp and groan, and when her hand finally touched him, he clenched his teeth so that they should have shattered.

Having ensured her protection, he moved over her, and she welcomed him. Her hands on his sides tugged him to her, and she shifted her hips to accommodate him. He hesitated, his whole body shivering with hot need, but still he hesitated.

She reached down and placed him to her heating lure, and the breath whooshed from him. She lifted her hips, but she needed his help.

And yet he hesitated, suffering, not wanting to hurt her.

She wrapped her arms around him and tried to do it herself, but she couldn't. "Oh, Quint, please."

Holding his breath, he pressed into her, then slid easily, deep inside. He raised himself up on his elbows, and he immediately put his hands to the sides of her face and peered at her, his concern for her had cooled him somewhat. "You okay?"

She was amazed. "You fit."

"Sure."

"Sure! How calmly you say that. Have you ever looked at yourself? I suppose you would have to've looked, what with one thing or another but, Quint, you're . . . well, I just didn't think it would work."

"You didn't think it would work, and yet you went ahead, anyway?"

"Well, women have been doing this sort of thing for a while, so I assumed I'd survive."

"But you thought I'd hurt you, and you let me go ahead?" He was appalled.

"It wasn't that bad. It really wasn't bad at all. More of . . . a surprise."

"How did you last this long without trying it out? You're a hot woman."

"Am I really? How nice of you to say that. Could you tell that I wanted you all this time?"

"All along? Why the hell didn't you say so?"

"It didn't seem the ladylike thing to do."

"Don't wait to tell me when you want me. I won't think you're unladylike."

She laughed in a throaty way. "Are you still afraid of me? You may move now."

"If you're sure you're okay." His renewed need was making his stillness difficult.

"Oh, Quint, I love you."

"Thank God for that."

Her hands cherished him, moving in his hair, onto his shoulders, down his back to his hips. "Tell me what to do," she whispered.

He asked, "How did God ever let me find you?"

"I knew you were around, somewhere, and I was ready down in Texas the first time I saw you, you nerd. What took you so long?"

"I'm unsuitable for you."

That word was very familiar. She commented, "Balderdash."

He kissed her then for a long, poignant time. Then again, differently. His body began to love hers as he moved, and he listened to her sighs, feeling her response to him. When she began to twitch, he moved from her and grinned at her protest. "In a minute," he said. "In a minute. Don't be in such a hurry."

Her eyes were a little unfocused, her lips red and puffy, and she was rather pale. She was panting, and she swallowed loudly. "Quint..."

"You're beautiful." He'd flung back the blankets from their steaming bodies, and he moved his hand on her. He leaned to taste her here and there. His eyes were yellow flames. His movements were quick, feeling her, and his hands were hard. A small smile of pleasure curled his lips.

But she wasn't a woman to be denied, and she was learning rather quickly. She could do what he had done to her, and she did those things to him. She surprised him. He had been with women who were familiar with men, but while the actions were very similar, Georgina's touches and explorations were different, new.

She was sassy, interested and eager. She laughed and touched, teased and kissed. She made it impossible for him to prolong their mating. Still careful of her, he took her again, easing into her, but then he had to ride to her eagerness.

He could only try to pace her. She was wild, and they clung, gasping, as they quickly made the zenith, hung there, and seemed to shatter before they fell back to reality, helpless. To murmur, their sweat intermingled, their spent bodies fused in tremors.

He managed to brace himself on his forearms to take some of his weight from her, but it was a while before he could summon the strength to move and collapse beside her, to his back, inert.

"My word," she said. "How amazing." And she added "Wow." She leaned up over his helpless mass. "That was marvelous. Do you realize we could have done this in Sacramento if you hadn't been so reticent?"

He smiled a little but didn't reply.

She rubbed the hair on his wide chest and said, "You're so much more *interesting* than I— "

He managed to make a dissenting sound.

"And I love your hairy body." She grinned, then put back her head and laughed. "You wear too many clothes."

"So do you," he mumbled.

"Well, if you think I'm going to parade around in this weather without any clothes on at all, you're mad."

He didn't respond.

"Since you're such an oven, it would be all right for you to go around naked."

His mouth stretched in a tiny grin, but his eyes remained closed.

She lay her chest on his and hugged him.

Slowly, heavily, his arms moved to enclose her, and having accomplished that, he went to sleep. She didn't move for a long time. But eventually she had to—she was turned wrong and her muscles were cramped. She carefully slid from him to lie beside him, and he shifted to accommodate her, still holding her in his arms.

Was he that used to sleeping with a woman? He wasn't even awake, yet he automatically moved to make her comfortable beside him. She frowned. But he'd told the skiers that he was pure. How could a pure man be unsuitable? He suited her just fine. She swirled her head so that she could look into his face. He was out cold.

She sighed in great contentment. There was no other place that she wanted to be right then but here—in this cabin, in Quint's bed, in his arms.

That brought to her mind the reason they were in that place, and she wondered who had taken the pictures of her. Who were those men on the snowmobiles, and who were the skiers?

While she was wondering about all those other people, she was ignoring the fact that she knew nothing about Quintus Finnig, this "unsuitable" stranger. Ah, but he was so gentle. He'd just about sweat blood over her having had no experience. If she hadn't been positive about continuing, he would have left her untouched. That showed the man he was.

And he had given Tate the pictures of her stolen son. Then he'd contrived with Tate's ex-husband to release the child and give Benjamin back to Tate. Georgina would remember that all her life.

A street child, Quint had called himself. She longed to know what had happened to him, why he'd been left to roam free, unprotected and alone. He was a puzzle, and she would solve him—this man, her man, her lover, her unsuitable love. Unsuitable? Phooey.

When Quint stretched and yawned, he realized Georgina was next to him. She grinned as he sucked in his beath in surprise. How often had he dreamed of her in his bed?

"Aren't you used to wakening to company in bed?" she asked saucily.

"No." He pulled her closer and hugged her tightly, moving his head so that he could find her mouth and kiss her.

"Where is the reticence? Where is the careful man who was reluctant?" She laughed, then tsked as he single-mindedly pursued his goal. "How shocking. You animal. Don't you kiss me there!"

"No?"

"Well, maybe..."

"Here?"

"Ooh..." she replied in an indrawn breath.

It was a while before they thought of supper. The fire had died almost to embers, and they had to coax it into a blaze again. They had wine with their contrived meal, and they were very mellow.

The wind had picked up. There was ice mixed in the snowfall. The radio said it would be partly cloudy with a few flurries that night and the next day. The lovers turned the radio to an FM music station, and settled down to talk.

"When did the mysterious strangers send you my pictures?" she asked.

"About a week ago. I'd have been here sooner to fetch you, but the day I'd planned to pick you up, you went skiing. That was a nuisance. It took some patched planning. Not being in a crowded place, like in a city, put a new slant on the requirements." He grinned at her. "You're worth it."

"Because I tumbled into your bed?"

He gave her a steady look. "Don't undervalue yourself. You gotta know what I mean."

She smiled at him, and he reached over to pull her onto his lap.

Seven

———

They had been at the cabin for twenty-four hours, and now there was time for them to talk. Sitting on Quint's lap, Georgina curled against him, her head on his shoulder, contented. She was sure they couldn't leave in the storm whose deep sounds were ominously thrilling.

But while she was contented, he was oddly restless. "Relax," she said in amusement.

"I feel like I ought to be patrolling."

"No one will be out in this storm. This will be a killer."

He reminded her, "The radio said partly cloudy."

"They always say that just before a killer storm. Don't you read any books at all?" He'd read that whole wall of books.

"I'm a city man. It's weird to be in a place with no people. It's empty. It's all just...landscape. Nobody's here."

She smiled deliciously. "All the world works their fingers to the bone to get enough money to buy a place off in the country, to get away from the city and be alone. All except Quintus Finnig. He wants people."

"People, I know."

"Ah. And do you know very many people?"

"When I was growing up," he explained, "I made up my own family."

"Did you? Who?"

Mentally, he went over the variety of people who were part of his Chicago network. "Just people. People who like me and are glad to see me."

Georgina was touched. He was a street child who'd gathered friends. What sorts of friends? Winos? Prostitutes? Thugs? "Tell me your life's story."

"I grew up on the streets and learned a lot."

She waited. "And..."

"I met a lot of different people that were nice to me or knocked me around; and I found out people are the same underneath, as each other, no matter what they wear or how much they know or how much they have."

She nodded, agreeing. "I've seen that in my job. I've seen the most insecure people who have such clout and who are responsible for such profound things, and they are a shambles when it comes to talking to other people or facing a crowd."

"It wasn't a crowd. It was you that turned them to jelly."

"I love prejudice."

He hugged her tightly and kissed her squishily. Then he . . .

"No, no." She stopped his hands. "I want to hear your life's story." She pried herself free and moved to sit on the sofa beside him.

He refilled her wineglass, and she gave him a droll smile as she slowly shook her head in censure and she demanded: "Tell me."

Quint looked at her a little like she'd backed him into a corner. Then he sighed, knowing he'd have to tell her at least a part of it. He rubbed his face with big hard hands.

His reluctance made her frown with concerned interest.

As if the words were forced from him, he said, "I don't really want to talk about it. I had a tough time some ways and real luck in other ways. I didn't pay attention to what or why or how. I just got along, doing what I had to do. It was no big deal."

"What happened to your people?"

"I don't know."

She pressed him, "What do you remember before you lived on the streets? Someone had to've taken care of you as a little child."

"I was in a bunch of foster homes. I was a runaway. They put me in a detention home. But I got away from there, too. They said I was a loner, incorrigible, a nonconformist, a delinquent, a free soul or whatever, depending on who was in charge of my file at the time."

"Which were you?" She really wanted to know.

"Nothing. I just wanted to have control. I wanted to be able to decide. And I didn't like people who were dumb, telling me wrong things and threatening me."

"What wrong things?"

"That I should take things, that God was going to strike me dead. That a cop would kill me if I didn't do what I was told. At that time, I had a cop for a friend." Quint was silent, then he said, "He was a good man. Frank Quintus. I took his name." He sighed a long sad breath before adding, "Some bastard knifed him by mistake. The guy was high and thought Frank was a devil. Really wigged out."

Being a Lambert from a small, secure Texas town, Georgina really wasn't aware how other people lived. She groaned inside her heart for the young Quint.

He went on. "Then I met Simon Finnig. I got my other name from him. He was the blackest-skinned man I ever met. He was good to me. I had my own code of conduct by then—I was about ten. But Simon showed me different—what a man can do, and what he never does. Simon was one of the good ones. He saw to it I ate regular, and he didn't turn me in." There was another pause. "When I got older, he taught me about books. I hadn't listened before then."

"Where is Simon now?"

"He died. Peaceful. In bed. On the streets, that's almost unknown. Just having a bed to die in was something. He was already old when I first knew him. When I have real problems, I think how Simon would solve it. He had a way of taking a problem apart and worrying it until it gave up its core. Then it would be simple to see what had to be done. You could solve it or give it up."

"So you chose your names from your friends."

"Yeah. They were good men."

"What was your real name?"

"Tom Brown."

After a while, Georgina told him, "I'm having trouble with the idea of you having been cold and hungry and lonely."

"I don't remember being lonely. I had a code that was mine. I had my territory. I watched everything in that area—who ought to be there, who was a stranger and I knew what was going on. When I got older, I . . . interfered." He smiled.

"In what way?"

"I organized the area and initiated Simon's rules of order."

"You started being a bully."

He grinned down at her. "There was others that thought that way, too."

"Did you speak another language?"

He became still and a little stiff. "What makes you ask that?"

She felt the withdrawal and realized she'd offended him. "You choose your words with care." She didn't mention the variance in his choice.

"I clean up the words." Quint couldn't bring himself to tell her he was trying to speak well for her.

Making amends, Georgina smiled up at him. "You don't have to be that careful around me. I can handle an occasional *damn* and *hell*. I have been known to use those myself, but not at home."

"You shock me, Miss Lambert."

She laughed, doubting that anyone could really shock him. What a strange life he'd led, and she wondered if she'd ever know his whole story.

"It's your turn. Tell me about Georgina Lambert of Texas."

"You've met us all. My parents are special. You know Tate. Being the eldest of five daughters, she influenced us greatly. All but Hillary still talk about Tate's Tarzan period. Fred was Jane. She's just two years younger than Tate, and Tate dominated her the worst of all. Fred did as she was told all through her childhood and has never learned to assert herself. Roberta is two years younger than I, and she mostly stood around in the face paint that Tate thought a native should wear. Roberta remembers that time as a dead bore. I loved Tate's Round Table era the best. I was the Black Knight. When you came to the lodge all dressed in black with that helmet, I thought of you as a Black Knight, unknown and dangerous."

"By now, you got to know I won't hurt you."

"I know. I liked being the Black Knight. That beat being Cheetah all hollow and—"

"Cheetah?"

"Uh-hmm. During Tate's Tarzan period. Outside of being a native, there was a limited choice. Hillary was youngest, so she had to be Boy, Tarzan's found child. Fred was Jane; I got to be Cheetah because I could climb the mulberry tree and hang by my hands. Tate bragged about that so much that I was proud of it.

Tate's a manipulator. We mostly stood around where Tate put us, and Tate told us the story and had great adventures while we watched. We had some very patient dogs and a lot of room."

"All of you are very feminine."

"Just think what pills we would have been without Tate's influence."

"Pills?"

"Pansies. Tate made us brave. Except for Fred. She's a wimp."

"She didn't seem that different."

"She's still waiting for Sling to propose."

"Waiting?" Quint considered her word. "What would you do in her place?"

"I wouldn't be sitting around waiting for directions from Tate. Hey! Maybe that's what Fred needs! She needs Tate to tell her how to make Sling make up his mind. When we get away from here, I'll call Tate and suggest it."

Rather droll for him, Quint said, "So you have some of Tate's instincts for controlling people."

"When you ignored me in Sacramento, I wished for Tate to come and tell you to talk to me, to touch me and make love to me as it was written in the script. I had no idea what to do about you."

"I did."

She gave him a darkling glance. "It took you long enough."

"I'd only seen you a couple of times. I didn't know it was the same with you as it was with me. When I saw you that first time, I was paralyzed."

"You gave no indication at all."

"I gave the pictures of Benjamin to Tate," he said, as if it was an explanation.

"What had you planned to do with them?"

"I need to get some name-backing. I thought Bill might come through with some clout if I used the pictures of Benjamin. But I saw you, and all my planning went up in smoke."

"You'd planned to bribe Bill?" She thought about that. "He'd probably have done it, he loves Tate so much."

"As I love you."

Naturally she had to ask, "Would you allow someone to use you for my sake?"

Simply, Quint confirmed it. "I gave him the pictures, no strings."

"Even if you'd used the pictures as you intended, you would still have won the hearts of the whole family. Benjamin's the only grandchild, and we missed him so badly. We lost two years of knowing Benjamin."

"People can be very unintentionally cruel," Quint explained kindly.

"You think Dominic wasn't deliberate in keeping Benjamin from Tate?"

"He's a possessive man. He thought it'd be better if Benjamin wasn't torn between two parents. He thought he was doing what was best for everybody. He hadn't counted on Benjamin remembering Tate the way he did."

Georgina told Quint gently, "You're a fine man."

"No." Again Quint felt the need to be entirely honest with her. "You gotta remember that I would have used the pictures of Benjamin to get to Bill. I'd have traded. It was you that made me give them as a gift.''

"Accepted.''

He wanted to be sure she fully understood how devious he'd been because of her. ''You know I did it to look good to you?''

''You looked good to me from the first glimpse. You're magnificent.''

''Georgina, I'm not good enough for you.''

She laughed in teasing and agreed. ''Probably not. You can work the rest of your life trying to convince me.''

He put his hand on her nape and shook her gently. ''You're a siren—one of the women that tempt men to run their ships on the rocks and drown.''

''I'd see to it that you didn't drown.''

His voice a little roughened by his emotion, he pushed it, saying, ''But you want to wreck me.''

''Not at all. I just wanted you to notice me.''

''I sure as hell did that.''

''See? You can speak comfortably with me.''

He laughed in black humor that she thought he could be comfortable with her in any way. ''Tell me how you landed in Sacramento, teaching tongue-tied men to talk to you.''

''I was in theater and speech in school. But acting jobs are few and far between. I was doing all sorts of temporary work. Do you know I was approached to pose for nude pictures and do skin—''

''You didn't.'' He was quite intense.

"A Lambert? You josh. Even as the Black Knight, I would have been drummed from the corps. Anyway, I met a nice man, Bob Johnson, and he was interested in starting a business in media training. I was qualified. He hired me. It's worked out well."

"What's this Bob like?"

She swallowed a smile. "A very kind, family man."

"He ever . . . come on to you?"

"Surely there can be no question in your suspicious mind that I've not played around."

"Yeah."

She tilted her head, keeping her gaze on him. "Are you a possessive man?"

"Compared to me, Dominic is a pussycat."

"Good gravy, what have I gotten into?"

But he took her seriously. "You need to know."

"You have no worries. We Lamberts are faithful."

"So am I."

He'd run the words together in his real speech. Georgina was especially touched because the words were so serious for him that he hadn't chosen them for effect but had said them naturally.

Their exchanged look was very serious. Then she smiled a little. "Do I get to sleep on the sofa?"

Quint was unfamiliar with gentle teasing, but he wanted to learn how to tease with Georgina. "You want us both to try to sleep on this sofa?" he asked carefully.

"No. I believe I'll sleep on the bed—" she drew it out "—as I did last night."

He laughed as she admitted knowing he'd switched her around. Did she also realize he'd known she was

awake then? He waited but she was being flippant, and
he relished watching her flirt with him. When had any
woman flirted with him? Would he have been interested enough to notice if they had? What woman had
he ever wanted to flirt with him? None. But he wanted
Georgina to flirt and tease him. He loved being lured
this way—gently, easily, sweetly.

Fate had given him this time with her through the
damnedest series of screwups possible. If his rescue
had gone as planned, they'd have been in Chicago
long before now, and he would have deposited her
with Bill and Tate or with Hillary and Angus. Instead, here she was with him, becoming increasingly
more snowbound in an isolated cabin. What had he
ever done in his life to deserve this gift?

But he didn't want her just for now; he wanted her
permanently. Could he manage that? Could he have
her forever? Never before had he wanted a woman
who was his.

He reached to unbutton her shirt. She watched his
hands work, then looked up into his face, smiling a
little, looking pleased, and his hands began to tremble. No other woman had ever affected him as she did.
Never before had his hands fumbled or shaken as they
did with her. And he'd thought he'd experienced passion. Nothing compared to what he felt with Georgina.

Now he could understand men who avoided women
whom they could love. He'd once heard a man say he
didn't want to see a particular woman again because
he could be too serious about her. Quint knew more
than one man who only had women around for the

purpose of having one but they avoided becoming attached to one. Quint had thought it was smart, because a woman could be a nuisance, but now he understood all of it. A man who loved a woman cared first for her. Nothing else was as important to him. That was how it was now for Quint. Only Georgina mattered. She was the danger he'd feared to his life and to his plans.

His plans had been primary to him, but now he was only interested in them. He wanted to be with Georgina. Would it last? After he'd had her for a while and they had become familiar, would he be able to turn from her and continue on as he had? Could he relegate her to being only a part of his life?

If she should take a primary part in his life, it would change. How? He stopped undressing her and just sat and looked at her, pondering the problem as Simon would have advised.

Did she sit still for that? No. She reached out and began to undress him. She did that with busy concentration, with an occasional chewed lip, a couple of licked lips, glances at him that smiled and flirted. And he knew he was lost.

When they were naked, she made him get into bed to warm it. Then, while he watched, she went around turning off lights and setting the fire for the night before coming to the bed. "Shall I lift you and carry you over to the sofa now? Isn't it time for me to have the bed? You've been in it long enough."

And he said, "You can try."

"I believe I've read that someone smaller than you can carry you with the fireman's hold. So it shouldn't be a problem. I can do anything."

She lifted the blankets, but before she could blink, he had pulled her into bed and had her pinned there with an arm and a strong, muscular thigh. "Is this street-fighting?" she inquired.

The contrast of actual street-fighting and being in bed with Georgina made him laugh.

She laughed with him. "How did you learn to make love?"

"Simon warned me about it. He told me a woman would come along who'd be the one I'd want, and I wasn't to fool around."

"Are you going to fool around with me?"

"No," he said soberly. "With you, I'm going to make love."

That's what he did. He made love with her, and she helped. Her introduction had been so amazing, but this was marvelous. He knew where she wanted to be touched, and he did that.

So she used him as a teacher and copied him. She had him in knots, and that was heady. But then he retaliated, using skills, and he had her sensitive body writhing, figuratively climbing up a high wall—that helpless, that excited, that insecure and needing much more, and a lot of help—which he gave her.

How different it was for him to make love with this woman. Why should it be? She was female, with the usual parts. Why was it so...enticing to touch her? For her to touch him? Why did her squeaks and gasps thrill him so much? Other women had writhed in his arms and made similar sounds. Why was this one so special?

And she was. To make love with her was awesome. She was what that misused word was meant to describe. She was awesome. Everything about her—from her soft lips and soft breasts to her hot lure and her sweet touch. Georgina. He loved her with his soul.

As his scorching hands searched her out and his scalding mouth suckled her, she could not control her small twistings and twitches. Her legs were restless and impatient and her hands urged him and she felt odd.

The friction of hair-textured flesh was exciting to her body, and she rubbed against him to feel his difference. She sighed, and her breath was broken as the ache built that only he could cure. And in that primitive cabin in the middle of a roaring storm, she became a primitive. And she set him on fire. They became so hot that the blankets were thrown back and still they heated.

She pushed against him until he lay back, allowing it, and she climbed on top of him, fit him to her, and rode him voluptuously. But he kept his big hands on her hips, and he controlled her, not allowing her release. She panted in frustration as he lifted her from him and lay her on his body.

Then he began to teach her other pleasures. His kisses changed and they made love at his pace. His searing tongue leisurely explored her ears as his hot hands moved down her back, and his fingers would reach farther to caress. He would couple with her and move exquisitely, then separate and rest, prolonging their loving. She became malleable and pliant. He did not.

Finally they could no longer control their passion, and they were pulled into the spiral that had lured them all along. They ascended to that peak of thrilling pleasure and reached ecstasy, as if it were a lightning rod in that storm, and they whirled away into oblivion. For they almost lost consciousness in their turmoil of pleasure.

He covered them with the blankets and folded her into his arms. Then they slept.

Several hours later, toward dawn, they awakened to the wind buffeting the snug cabin. Quint got up and put more logs on the fire. Then he returned to bed and took her back against him.

His big hand smoothed her blonde hair away from the pale oval of her face and he could see her smile. "It's different with you."

"Is it?"

"It's never been that way," he said solemnly.

Since she had no idea that was profound, she replied, "You are fantastic. We could make a fortune with you if I was more open-minded."

"Are you possessive?"

She agreed. "But I never was before now."

"Then you love me."

A little sassily, she said, "I told you that."

"Tell me again."

She shook her head. "I don't think I should. You'll get a swelled head and—stop that!—and I'll—do be serious—I'll have a time getting you to behave."

"How do you want me to behave?"

Elaborately, she pretended to think. "Mmm, I'll have to decide."

"I'll do anything for you."

"I think a drink of water would help. You've had me trapped in this bed for a week."

"Does it seem a week to you?" he asked as he released her and got up. "I feel like it's been only minutes."

"Yes. But doesn't it seem like an age since we left the lodge on that motorcycle? What happened to Dave and that other man, do you suppose? And to Frances's ski suit?"

He brought back a glass of water and handed it to her. "I don't know about the ski suit, but the guys'd be okay. Whoever is after us must have one hell of a lot of people to spread out the way they did."

She quit drinking to comment, "From what I've heard, when Tate was missing, *you* had people spread out all over Chicago."

"Nothing surprising. Just people I know."

"No one has that many people to tap."

He explained, "I've been in business in Chicago for a lot of years. I've made a lot of contacts. People are willing to help in emergencies."

"How are we an emergency to someone out here so that a person can call in so many people to search for us?"

He sighed. "I hope we're in Chicago when we find out."

"Why Chicago?"

"I got people there I can trust."

She handed him the empty glass. "What about those you know here? How do you know them?"

"I was in business with them some time back."

"I know I'm not the one who interests them. What do you do that's a threat to someone out here?"

He took the glass back to the counter, then turned to look at her. "I'm clean."

"Have you always been?"

"No drugs, no prostitution, nothing mean."

"But something illegal?"

He came back to the bed. "It all depends on which side of the fence you're on. But I'm legit."

"You don't intend telling me."

He put a hand on her head and shook her head a little. "It's best for you not to know everything about me." He got back into bed.

"You think I'd . . . spill the beans?"

"There's no point. It's all past."

She frowned, trying to figure him out. "What on earth?"

"Nothing . . . now. I just don't want you disillusioned."

"You're a good man."

"Hold the thought."

"I have a curious streak this wide," she declared, a little exasperated.

"I've done nothing to shame you."

But she wasn't satisfied and said only, "Curiouser and curiouser."

"Are you hungry?"

"I believe I could be coaxed."

He slid her over him and lifted the covers for her to get out of bed. "Call me when breakfast is ready."

"Aha! So you're that kind of a man."

"It's good for you to know it right away, so you have no illusions."

Sitting on the side of the bed, she put her hands to her head and said dramatically, "The thrill is gone."

"Careful."

She turned toward him and looked down into his interested face. "Drama turns you on?"

"*You* do."

"Oops, sorry." She jumped out of reach and looked back. As he folded his hands behind his head and smiled a little, she wondered again if no one had ever teased him. So she gave him a disdainful snub and walked regally toward the bathroom.

Quint's face softened. She was so elegant. He lay there listening to the sounds of the shower—and her shriek! He leaped from the bed to meet her at the bathroom door.

Indignantly, she told him, "There's no hot water!"

He didn't actually smile but he was excellent in his reply, "How barbaric."

And she laughed.

If he hadn't loved her before then, that would have done it.

Eight

There's nothing worse than a pampered woman," Quint said with an indulgent smile, as he heated water on the stove for Georgina. There was bottled gas for that purpose. They were surprised that it took longer for water to boil at that altitude.

They sponge bathed their sticky bodies. He offered to help her, but she blushed and declined. She turned her back and was modest. His familiarity with her was too new for him to be too forward or bold. But he couldn't control his glances. He knew how to look without seeming to, and he filled his soul with her form, her movements, her grace, the beautiful feminine curve of her spine.

His ears absorbed any sound she made, he was so conscious of her; but he controlled his hands. They reached automatically toward her, and he had to keep his arms tensed in order to prevent his hands from constantly touching her.

Outside, the storm raged; and the two fugitives opened the barred shutters to be confronted with absolutely nothing but swirling wind-driven snow. They added wood to the faithful fire and settled down to fix an elaborate lengthened breakfast.

"Have you ever been snowbound?" she asked with a casualness that revealed only an inkling of her avid curiosity about him.

"No."

"Now, I happen to know that Chicago has had a blizzard or two. Tate has lived up there for just over five years, you know, and she's told of one that stopped everything—uh—cold."

"If it's necessary, a man can get through anything."

She studied him. "So?" she teased. "Just what was it that made you get out in the last blizzard?" Then she sat back, waiting to be entertained.

Quint was a while in replying. He was committed to telling her what truth he could, so he was honest, and that made him uncomfortable. "There was people that had to have help."

Georgina's expression changed a little. She should have guessed that. He'd had a "territory" when he was ten. That feeling of proprietorship would not have lessened in the past twenty-eight years of overseeing other lives. Basically, he was an Irish king.

"You supplied food?"

"Worse. They needed heat. We had to get them collected and to another place. People have it tough."

Yes, she thought, some did have it tough. But they had Quint and he would take care of them. If she were sick and cold, she would want him. She looked at him with tenderness. She would want him just as badly if she were well and warm. "How did you manage?" she asked.

"I was one of a lot of other people. The churches help. The city does its damnedest. Everybody helps. In bad times people forget the differences—they pay attention about others. I was just one of the mob."

"There first."

"I'm bigger and my legs're strong. I could get through." His eyes were seeing inwardly. "I know where to look."

She understood this ex-street child. He would know where to look; he'd been there. She was again swamped with compassion for the child who'd been so alone. "I wish you'd never had to live that way."

His expression showed surprised. "It was a great adventure. I ran my own life. Especially after Simon saw to it that I ate regular, it was great."

How incredible. Then Georgina remembered John Boorman's book HOPE AND GLORY. It involved his memories of being nine years old in nightly bombed London during World War II, and his great adventures in the rubble. The searchlights, flak and barrage balloons were the "fireworks" of the night. Life, good or bad, mostly depended on one's point of view. And Quint's memories weren't bitter. Life had been an adventure.

She knew then that for Quint, the Irish king, a territory would be enough. It could be run his way and he could see to it that his subjects had care. He was a nurturer, this "unsuitable" man. She reached her hand out and laid it on his arm.

He immediately covered her hand with his and never noticed he'd dropped his fork, in the doing of it. His gaze intense, he said, "You touched me."

"I need permission, sire?"

"No." His reply was instant. His glances were quick and searched her face, her eyes, her mouth. "Why did you call me that?"

She tried to remember what she'd called him.

"Why did you call me 'sire'?"

"I believe you should have been an Irish king." She smiled at her flight of fancy, but he stared at her. He probably thought she was silly.

As he stared at her, in his mind he saw himself, leaning from a very large white horse, lifting Georgina from her family's collective clutching hands and riding away with her, across a green land, toward a castle far away from them all. He had never ridden a horse, but in this time he had other means of transportation. He would steal her from them.

He thought that would be a solution—to steal her away. He hadn't stolen anything since he'd made Simon so mad. But Georgina would be worth the risk. Would she be willing to be stolen? He couldn't do it against her will. If she was willing, it wouldn't be stealing. It was only her family who wasn't willing. She loved him. He lifted her hand from his arm, his gaze holding hers, and he kissed her palm. "If I was a king, I'd want you to be my queen."

"I'd be honored."

"Oh, Georgina," he groaned. Then he stood and lifted her in his arms. He just wanted to carry her around again, to hold her, to feel her slight weight and her softness against his body, to have her in his possession.

Georgina thought how physical he was. When he seemed content to simply stand there with her in his arms, she said, "I haven't finished my breakfast."

He gave her a sharp look, then his eyes sparkled. "How can you think of food at a time like this?"

"Easily. My desire is sated, I've had enough sleep, but my stomach is empty. I'm hungry."

"Simon always said that women were different, but I didn't know what he meant. I thought it was in physical appearance. I'd noticed that. But this weird thing about eating instead of letting me carry you around is different. Selfish," he judged.

"Come on, you big lug. Put me down."

"Oh, all right." He sighed as if much put-upon.

She realized that for him, this was the beggings of teasing. She ruffled his hair and kissed his chin. He made his mouth available but she dodged and went back to the table.

Her egg was dead cold. They had waffles next, and as they ate, she told him freely about her own life, and gradually dug clues from him about his own.

She was fascinated that he didn't feel the least bit deprived, even though he'd never had a happy home. That made her wonder if he could live a normal family life...with children of his own. But it was too early in their relationship to broach such a subject. She knew his answer would be important to her. She looked at him, imagining the sort of rebellious, arrogant sons he'd have, and how he might cope with them. Probably roaringly. She smiled.

"Why're you smiling?"

"I was wondering what sort of children you would have."

He assumed she worried about being pregnant. "We were careful."

"I know that."

"I'd marry you." He was earnest. "I'd do what was right."

She touched his cheek to acknowledge his concern. "I was wondering about your kids—how they'd look."

"I got no kids. They'd be ugly. I've been called an ugly Mick all my life." He dismissed the subject and went back to his waffles.

She put down her fork, got up and wiggled her hips between him and the table to sit on his lap. He helped, enclosing her in his arms, putting his face against her soft breasts with a groan of pleasure.

"Cut that out!" she scolded, very pleased. "All that I'm trying to do is see if you're really an ugly Mick." Busily she put her hands on the sides of his head and tilted his precious face up to hers. His face was grim; his eyes sad.

Quint was embarrassed but held still for her examination. He took her seriously. He figured she might just as well realize he was ugly now, when her initial sexual attraction was new and distracting her. And if she really loved him, then by the time she realized how ugly he was, she might love him enough to accept him.

Georgina smiled at him tenderly as she cataloged his face. "Even features. Thick eyebrows. I like that kind. How nice you don't have to paste on more in order to please me. I wish I had your eyelashes." She was touching as she went along. "Yours are gorgeous. So thick and black. Beautiful. Aesthetically, your jaw is a little stubborn." She pulled back as if in surprise. "Are you stubborn?"

Mesmerized by her, flattered, believing her every word, Quint shook his head, denying stubborn.

She laughed over that and he wasn't sure why. So he just enjoyed the sound of her laughter, the feel of her sitting on his lap, her attention concentrated on him. The women who'd sat on his lap generally wanted something from him. What did Georgina want? She could have his soul. It was all he possessed that was worth anything. He knew it would be safe in her keeping.

She had her hands in his hair and was petting him. Loving that, he understood cats better. He felt like purring and rubbing against her. So he did, and he was rewarded with her deliciously intimate laugh. He nuzzled his face against her softness, his breathing quickening.

She scolded, "If you hide your face, I can't tell if you're really ugly or if you're setting me up to kiss you and make you into a prince."

This time he recognized the teasing. He wished to God his tongue was clever. He stumbled over the words. "We could try. There has to be some truth in fairy-tales." And as she laughed so softly, he felt a cleverness nothing else had given him. He was elated.

She turned his face to hers and looked at it with amused eyes. Her fingers smoothed his hair back and her hands cupped the back of his head. "You've been trying to hornswoggle me—"

"'Hornswoggle?'"

"—into believing any Irishman would ever consider himself less than perfect. Your breed, sire, is notoriously vain. Since they know they are perfect, they pretend flaws so that they can coax innocent bystanders into assuring them they are, indeed, perfect. You're just as bad as all the rest."

He listened, and his mouth opened in astonishment. "You say...you mean...you think...I'm not...ugly?"

Appalled he'd been so insecure, Georgina managed a good chuckle. Tightening her fingers in his hair, she shook his head a little. "See? An insatiable appetite for praise. Okay. I'll tell you every twenty-four hours, but no more than that, okay? You're a damned good-looking man. You must have to brush women off constantly. You are built like a dream man and you move like a very dangerously exciting one. You're squeezing the air out of my lungs, sire, and if I can't breathe, I can't... That's better. How have you escaped marriage this long?"

"I hadn't found you yet."

She sobered as she said, "Yes."

"I can't keep my hands off you."

"I like to be touched by you."

"I'll have to grow another pair of arms and hands."

"Where? From the elbow?"

"No, that would limit my reach." When she laughed, he smiled to hear it. He realized he was pleased beyond sense to delight her and to make her laugh. He hugged her to him in an agony of uncertainty. How long would he have her within his reach? He could talk of sharing his throne of her imagination, but any thought of permanence in their relationship, or marriage, was built of equal foolishness. As impossible. But the thought of giving her up went through him like a soul-killing pain.

"It's my waffles that are getting cold this time. I'll lose weight and waste away with your distracting me this way. I need to eat."

Without loosening his arms, he raised his face that bit to look into her eyes. Then he released one of his hands with some humorous effort, as if he was made of metal and she was a magnet. He pulled her plate over to them and gave her his reconstituted orange juice.

She sipped the juice, then judiciously shared the rest with him. With her hands free and his so involved, she fed him some of her cold waffles, which were ambrosia to his tongue. As she busily blotted his lips, she commented with a clinical interest, "I don't recall sitting on too many laps, but I am somewhat startled to discover, sire, that you may well be growing an extra limb."

She sat back sassily with slightly raised brows and waited. She saw his pupils flare, then the humor sparkle there. He did try not to laugh. He cleared his throat and turned his head aside to cough, and then he laughed. Such a silly thing, but she'd finally made him laugh. She laughed along, enormously pleased.

As his laughter eased, he took her shoulders in his big hands and shook her the tiniest bit. He scolded in delight, "You know what happens to wicked women who tease a man that way?"

She straightened, put both hands up to her head to help her thinking process as she concentrated on the answer to his question. "She gets to go out into the raging blizzard and get more wood?"

"Guess again."

"Uh," Georgina stated in mock disgust, "she has to do the dishes?"

"She takes off that T-shirt and those baggy panties and gets back into bed."

"By this time, that bed is freezing and—"

"I'll get you warm soon enough."

"See?" She stood up and pulled the T-shirt over her head. As her tumbled hair fell back to her shoulders, she went on complaining: "Arrogance. Just exactly what I thought from the first time I saw you, you Irish king, you. A woman makes a perfectly innocent observation and you have to show her what happens next." She paused. "You don't believe in just telling a woman what could happen?"

"No."

Standing there in baggy panties and a lot of uncovered skin, she put her hands on her hips and flung back her hair in a very tempting way. "You use that word a lot, do you know that, you arrogant Irish king?

Can't you ever say 'yes'?'' she asked, leading him into joining her sassiness.

The fires of passion were leaping in his eyes and his head was a little forward on his formidable shoulders. He watched her so intently that he excited her, but he didn't reply.

Deliberately she moved, flinging out a hand, knowing she was showing off, tempting him and flirting. "'Yes' is quite easy to say, you know." She went to him, pinched his lips together to form an exaggerated baby-bird mouth and said a slow, "Y-y-y-e-s-s-s."

He kissed her as she knew he would. But then she had to work to pull away enough to praise him. "Excellent!" she bragged. "That shows a willingness to cooperate. Let's see if we can get the actual word from you. Practice always improves performance, don't you agree?"

He smiled.

She raised her brows. "Should I remove the baggy panties?" She hooked her thumbs into the slack waistband and waited expectantly, encouragingly.

His chest rumbled with his humor and he managed to reply an excellent "Yes."

She took her thumbs from the lax waist of the panties in order to clap her hands and praise him, "Marvelous!"

Then she went on chatting. "I knew if you just tried you could say something besides that tiresome 'no' you stick into the conversation. I am so excited you managed the 'yes' because you must have a dreadfully packed store of them just waiting—"

"I said *yes*, that I want you to take off those panties."

She looked down past her peaked breasts and feigned surprise to see the panties still hung on her hips. "These?"

He smiled wickedly. "Yes."

She celebrated. "You did it again. How exciting for you! It's always exhilarating to learn a new skill and—"

"Take them off."

Stopped mid-clap, her forearms covered her breasts and she looked around inquisitively. "Take 'them' off? What?" She looked back to him with an attentive face.

"You asked me if you oughta take off those panties, and I said yes."

She flung out a hand in a dismissive gesture, revealing one naked breast. She said in realization, "Oh. Well, yes, I did ask you that question, but it was a survey sort of thing and I didn't say anything about actually—"

"Are you teasing me?"

In order to reply, she had to clarify the question. "Am I teasing you? Hmm." While she pondered that, she stretched her arms up, moved around and bent over as she made sounds of cogitation. She was amazed he kept his distance. At last she turned back to him, and she understood that his question had been serious. He wasn't sure she meant to tease him, and he was leashing himself as he waited for her reply.

Impudently, she again stood before him, moving enough to make her naked breasts shimmer. "May I unbutton your shirt?"

He was in torment. His eyes watched her avidly. "My God, Georgina," he murmured.

A stickler, she said, "I have to have the actual word here, and it's *yes*."

"Yes."

"Very good! That's at least four that you've managed to say. Perhaps I can help you get rid of some more?"

Quint couldn't reply.

So, still wearing the droopy panties, she went near him and slowly reached out to unbutton his shirt. She did that insidiously, her fingers slipping inside and touching against his furry chest as she turned her head just a little, chewed on her lower lip and licked her upper one.

Quint held still for it. In an agony of desire, he learned about temptation. He hadn't realized how wonderful a woman could be. Not really. He'd only known the need for release. He watched Georgina, so thrilled by her. It was almost too much. He was peeled from his clothes, and it was fortunate that she'd made love with him that morning, or he never would have lasted.

As she slid his pants down his hips, his eager sex leaped free. She drew back her head as if surprised, and she looked up into his eyes. Then she had the audacity to reach a finger out and tickle its bottom and the crazy thing went wild.

Before she knew it, her panties were on the floor and she was flat on her back, screeching about the cold bed, but then he kissed her. She mumbled protests through the first one, but she didn't say anything after the second one, and by the fifth one, somebody should have opened a window to cool off the room.

So after their nap, their interrupted breakfast had sort of run into lunch.

"We've done nothing but eat today," Georgina said.

Quint only smiled lazily. His appetites were large, as he was.

After eating, they did the dishes and tidied the room, straightening the bed. Quint thought that was a waste of time. They had made inroads on the wood-box, so they dressed in warm clothing, with Georgina in the mottled overalls. The snow deterred them from using the front door, so they went down the secret stairs, pulled back the bench and crawled along the tunnel to the shed.

It was exhilarating to be in the wind-buffeted shed and listen to the storm still blowing so wildly. The cabin was so solid and protected that the storm hadn't made a big impression on them. Now the fury of it was more audible, more obvious, and it was cold out there.

They each gathered an armload of wood, then saw a flat, round pan with a rope. Quint figured it was to pull along the tunnel, loaded with logs. It worked perfectly. After doing several runs, they latched the secret entryway with a sense of satisfaction. They'd thought the secret stair was for devious means of ingress and escape, but it was a practical one to get wood from the shed. And the shed was in case the house caught fire then, in just such a circumstance, there would be a shelter for survival.

They looked around their sanctuary and smiled at it and at each other. They agreed it was perfect. But then they thought the day was perfect, too. Since there was a storm raging outside, they realized that would cast some suspicion on how reliably they were thinking.

They had wine with their ham dinner, and whipped cream on their baked apple pie. They ate leisurely, and again, Georgina did most of the spasmodic talking. They were very comfortable together—or perhaps they were simply mellow, living in an unreal world.

After dinner, the dishes were put to soak. "Dishes need time to think about getting clean," Georgina explained. "It's traumatic for dishes to be washed too quickly." She was surprised Quint hadn't ever heard that.

"We didn't mess around with dishes too much on the streets."

"How practical. We may put the dishwashing soap dealers out of work."

They turned on the FM station and caught the disc jockey in the middle of a spiel. " . . . supposed to go south of here. I hope all you chillun are safe inside. Any of you who are stuck in snowbound cars, we'll be looking for you. Sorry about that. Here's two hours straight of cheerful tunes to keep you warm. I know. But it's the best we can do. Here's looking *for* you, kid."

The music was such a rhythmic lure that it wasn't long before Georgina was on her feet and moving to the beat. She wasn't trained, but she was naturally graceful. She was a sight to him and his focus never left her.

At last he couldn't resist and he stood as she smiled at him. He moved minimally but matched her rhythm, as would a drum to keep the beat. It was stirring to them. Their movements were something like the Hawaiian dancing. The graceful female counterpointed by the strong masculine movements in punctuation.

Although they slept sweetly in each other's arms, they didn't make love that night. Her needs had been soothed and she was contented; Quint contained his desires, worrying that she would be exhausted by him. They slept heavily and wakened to silence.

At first they were confused. Then Quint said, "The storm's past."

They opened the shutters and gazed out on a wonderland. The storm-curtain had been lifted away to reveal the obscured beauty of the land. It was all new again—the winds had been so strong that now there were bald spots where the deep snow had been scoured away from the land.

"Those are deer tracks in the yard," Georgina exclaimed. "What on earth are they doing still up here at this altitude?"

Quint had no idea. "The only deer I've seen was at the Brookfield Zoo in Chicago."

"It is so interesting, all that's being done to help animals survive. There are reserves now where endangered species are allowed to roam free in places as nearly like their native lands as they can be made. Since the animals feel that they're in their natural habitat, they breed. That way, we don't lose their kind."

"We ought to worry about the kinds of peoples," Quint said. "There are ... tribes that are being wiped out just like the animals and birds and things."

She was still thinking about animals. "At one time the whooping cranes numbered only seventeen. They're making a comeback. There still aren't enough to be relaxed about their survival, but there are more now than there were."

He looked at her and replied, "People oughta come first."

She blinked, then lectured, "Without the rest of the creatures, this would be a bleak and pitiful planet. There is a forest in the East where there is a caterpillar that lives nowhere else in all the world. And that forest is in jeopardy. The caterpillar has a substance that is of interest to medical research. If the forest is lost, the caterpillar is, too, and its essence is lost to all of us."

"I can't work up no worry about caterpillars."

"What peoples do you worry about? Those in your territory in Chicago?"

"Them, too."

The two so deep in conversation were city people used to traffic of all kinds so they hadn't really listened to the helicopter approach. Suddenly Quint looked at the ceiling as if he could see through it, and he said, "Get into your clothes. Be quick. Somebody's coming."

She scoffed. "They always go around looking out for people after a storm like that. They won't be interested in us unless they see a red flag out, or a message in the snow, or a smoldering house or a stranded car—something like that."

"Cut it out 'n do what I tell you. *Right now!*"

Nine

Georgina protested, "Quint, no one is coming here. They can see the house is standing, smoke is coming from the chimney, no sign of distress. No one will worry about us."

He took her arm in his big hand and said through gritted teeth, "Do as I said."

She was slow in obeying, because Quint took such interesting means to wipe out all traces of her presence in the cabin. He took her clothes to the bed and threw back the top blanket to lay the clothes evenly on the second blanket. Then he carefully pulled the top blanket up over them and it was as if she'd never been there.

She tried to scoff about any danger but the helicopter was hovering. So she did as she had been instructed, but she did it with a big, patient sigh and in an indulgent manner.

He took an extra comforter from the storage closet and opened the secret stairway. "Hurry!" he snapped at her.

She stumbled down the steps after him, protesting, "Quint—"

"There's a place in the shed between the wood stacks and the south window. It's big enough for you. It'll be cold. Wrap yourself up. When the chopper leaves, come back into the house. You'll be safe then. Murray will check on you in a week or so. Don't go outside until he comes. Do you understand? Don't go out when they've left."

He had moved the bench aside and now he pulled her to him and hugged her with such violent anguish that she was immobilized. Then he released her, saying; "Hurry! Get hidden before they land, and don't move until they've left."

"Who—"

But he had thrust her into the tunnel and swung the weighted bench back into place. She heard his steps go up the secret stairs and the clunk as the bookcase was closed. Then there was silence. No. There was the helicopter. It was closer. It was…landing? How strange. Why? Who?

It was only then that she understood. As incredible as it was, Quint had a formidable enemy—one who could command a helicopter in this pressured time, when all airborne vehicles would be searching for victims of the killer storm. If Quint was correct, the enemy was looking only for him. And he had no weapon and no backup.

He had her.

So she disobeyed. In the dark of the tunnel, she searched the back of the bench for the release that would let it swing aside. Instead she touched something that opened a recessed part on the tunnel-side of the bench. Her fingers recognized two hunting rifles hanging on a rack. On a ledge below the guns were shells.

Being a Lambert, she was familiar with guns through skeet shooting and target practice. She took the heavier gun and filled her right pocket with shells. She patted the other rifle and that's when she found a handgun. She put that in her other pocket with shells suitable for it.

She had become a war machine—Quint's backup. She would not allow anything to happen to him because now she understood that in order to protect her, he was going to pretend he was there alone. For whatever reason there could possibly be for it, Quint thought that these intruders could take him away or kill him and leave his body in the snow, not to be found until spring, if then. That was why he'd said she was not to leave the cabin until Murray came for her. That was why... She'd think about that later.

She found the release on the bench and crawled out into the basement, carefully clicking the bench back into place. She checked and loaded both guns, noting they'd been well cared for. Then she went up the stairs and listened at the closed bookcase. There was a pounding on the outside door and a muffled voice hollered, "We know you're there, Finnig. Open up."

A chill went through her. It was the final confirmation that Finnig was right. These were not rescue people, but people who had gone to great lengths to track Quint down. And in zips, she wondered who Quint was, and what he'd done to be hunted so inconveniently by helicopter in such weather.

But she also knew that she could allow no harm to come to him. She was committed to him. If he was running from the law, she would help see to it that he had a fair hearing, and she'd stand by him. But if it wasn't the law, then she would see to it that he survived, and she was prepared to do whatever that took.

Georgina didn't mull over the fact that she considered he could be in trouble with the law, or why, only that if it was true, she could accept it, and she would do what she could for him. It was a non-admitted acknowledgement that he was unsuitable. She disregarded that he was.

"Who wants me?" she heard Quint ask.

"Come out. He's in the chopper. Come out and he'll talk."

"I'm not carrying anything."

"We don't mind."

"Back away," Quint commanded.

"I gotta frisk you."

"I've told you I'm clean. Get away from the door."

There was a long silence. "Okay, but move slow. He wants to ask you a couple of questions."

Quint warned, "Stay where I can see you."

"Be careful. No fast moves."

Quint said, "I'm harmless."

The words caused the unknown voice to laugh harshly—not amused, but patently unbelieving.

The exchange proved to Georgina that it wasn't the law who had come for Quint. The law identifies itself and follows rules. Quint needed a gun.

Georgina reached to open the bookcase. Then she heard the front door open and, trying to hurry, she fumbled as she heard the struggle that was taking place at the opening of the door. They had attacked Quint! She blundered and the door didn't open immediately. Her breath was fast and uneven as her fingers scrabbled. She stopped, took a steadying breath, then found and released the latch and swung the bookcase open.

The cabin was empty and the door was wide open. That they couldn't even close the door spoke volumes about the men who had come. If they were that careless of heat in this weather, how careful would they be of Quint?

This was serious—that finally sank into Georgina's consciousness. She stared at her face in the mirror opposite the bookcases and she looked awful. She looked female and she looked pale and scared.

She'd abandoned the quilt in the tunnel. Her coveralls were mottled green, and her woolen cap was a black-blue knit. The problem was her betraying white blob of a face. She rushed to the fireplace, reached in, along the cool side, dragged her hand across the soot which she smeared on her cheeks, forehead and chin.

That was better. She looked like a pro. She tilted the gun up with familiarity and strode to the door. She

peeked out and saw that they had bound Quint's
hands behind his back and in the deep snow the two
men were shoving him through some thin trees toward the helicopter, which rested on a wind-scoured
spot a short distance from the cabin. There was a third
man inside the chopper, Georgina could see his silhouette.

For all she knew, they had a cannon on the chopper. She had to be in range of countering that. So she
slipped out the door, leaving it open in case they
glanced back, and ran to the shelter of the trees, hid-
ing, watching for her chance. She would capture them
all.

As the two men and Quint approached the chopper, the third man got out and stood down on the
ground. Quint had known he couldn't appear to be too
eager to meet whoever wanted to see him. But he
couldn't be too reluctant, or they would look around
and hunt down Georgina. Her safety came first.
Whatever happened to him, she must not be found.

Grousing, he had allowed them to bind him, so they
hadn't done it too tightly. They weren't gentle in
guiding his steps, but they were those kind of men.
With their macho self-image, they had to hustle and
push; it was to be expected. They had to look good to
their boss. Quint could understand that.

He didn't know the man who exited from the chopper, and he was curious. They were walking toward
him when off to his left he heard Georgina's voice
shout, "Freeze!"

His reflexes were automatic and he knocked into
both men to destroy their chance of immediately

shooting Georgina. In return, one hit him over the head with the barrel of his gun, but he'd stumbled from Quint's shove, so the gun's blow only glanced off his skull. He fell as Georgina loosed a barrage of very loud bullets from a gun much too large for her. All he could think was: my God!

He'd turned as he fell and looked at her through his snow-covered face. She had found the perfect spot— a forked tree that gave her a great deal of protection with a clear view of the chopper and all four people by it. She had the gun and cover; they were in full view. It was her hand.

In a Marine sergeant's voice she yelled, "I said 'freeze' and that means you don't move a muscle."

Nobody moved.

One thing about being a Lambert was that it never occurred to one that she wasn't in control. "Throw your guns twenty feet behind you. Now!" Georgina ordered.

They did that. Quint sweated. He knew no one of their kind carried only one gun.

"Who is she?" the boss asked him.

So Georgina could hear, Quint replied loudly, "That's the Black Knight."

One of the others said derisively, "In the snow you use white. You don't use stove blacking."

"She was trained in the jungles of Texas," Quint explained.

That appeared to satisfy them.

"Get away from Finnig," Georgina yelled. "You two, move! Get over by the chopper."

"Pay attention," Quint said quickly.

The two moved as directed.

The boss said to Georgina, "We just want to know why he's out here."

She replied coldly, "It's a free country. He can go anywhere he wants."

That brought an astonished silence.

"Did they hurt you?" she asked Quint.

"No problem."

"Can you get up?"

He rolled to his feet and stood.

"Can you free your hands?"

He calmly stepped back through his linked hands, then lifted them to his teeth and pulled the knot free. He eyed the three spectators. "Why are you here?"

Again the boss inquired, "What're you doing out here on the West Coast, Finnig?"

"Are you the one who sent the pictures?" Quint asked.

"We just wanted you to know we knew you'd been floating around out here."

"I was just checking on my personal interests. I didn't think anyone would notice."

"We knew when you left Chicago."

"I got no other interests out here," Quint assured him.

"We're happy to hear that. Why did you snatch her from the lodge?"

"What would you have done in my shoes?"

The boss shook his head. "I sure as hell wouldn't have ridden a motorcycle up those roads."

"Are my boys okay?" Quint asked, in a hard, tough way, his voice very soft.

The boss shrugged. "I hate to admit it, but they disappeared. They slipped away like smoke. Who the hell were they?"

"Only old friends," Quint assured him. "No threat to you."

"That truck was sneaky. How did you set it up so fast?"

Quint understood all the talk was only to let him know how much they knew of his movements. He shrugged. "That was a fluke. She went skiing at the last minute. We had to...ad-lib."

"What're your plans?" the boss asked.

"I'd like to take her back to Chicago with me. And if she comes back west, I don't want her bothered, at all."

"Done. We'll be passing the airport, if you want a lift?"

Georgina replied coldly. "I learned at my mother's knee that one never gets into a chopper with any man on whom one is holding a gun."

The boss appeared to sort that out in his mind before nodding.

Georgina was still holding the rifle when the three men lifted off in the chopper. She wouldn't allow them to retrieve their guns, and they appeared to understand about that. As the chopper disappeared, she turned to Quint and demanded, "Let me see your head." Obediently, Quint leaned over so that she could. She touched his head gently and said, "You'll have a bump."

"I'm okay," he told her. Then he looked at her and said huskily, "The Black Knight."

"That was exactly how I felt. I was scared to death you were going to be hurt. I'll bet you twenty cents those guns aren't registered."

"Really?"

She informed him, "Those men are crooks."

"I'll bet you're right."

"Quint, they called you by name. How did they know your name, and how did they know when you left Chicago?"

"I don't know."

"You aren't really answering me, you know."

He looked surprised. "I *don't* know."

"You're talking to me the way men talk to women when they have no intention of telling them anything. It's just a lot of words and you're not telling me anything."

"I don't know how they knew."

"Why would they worry about you being on the West Coast?"

Yet again, he said, "I don't know."

"Are you a crook?"

"No."

Georgina studied him. "I'm glad it wasn't the cops."

"Me, too. Thank you for rescuing me. You were...magnificent, and I could throttle you for not minding me. You scared me spitless."

She gave him a quelling sideways glance that should have frozen his soul. "I could handle it."

She filled his unfrozen soul with such a burst of tenderness that his eyes prickled. He said in a gruff voice, "You were scary with your face all red and black. You looked mean.

"I had decided to kill them if they weren't cops."

His eyes quit prickling but his scalp did. "You would have done that to save me?"

"Yes."

"I learned just lately that 'yes' answers are rewarded."

And there in the snow, he took her into his arms and kissed her as a man should kiss a woman under those circumstances: blazingly, possessively, consuming her.

They quarreled because Georgina wanted to know exactly why those men had hunted Quint down.

Quint said "There wasn't any reason."

She didn't believe him. She sulked and slept on the sofa. He took the bed, and that made her more angry. The lights were out, the fire banked, the room obscured in darkness.

She listened as he moved restlessly, trying not to make a sound. So it was his effort to be silent that reached her. He was considerate of her. Accepting that, she thought about all she knew of him. He had promised her the men had no call to look for him. He'd said he was clean. Why hadn't she believed him? She had not—and she was embarrassed by her conduct.

She lay silently, curled on her side, watching the banked logs glow and spark, and she thought about Quint, the man who owned her heart. She saw him again as he'd appeared each time she'd been with him, and she recalled his few words as she watched him in her mind. He was a man.

He'd remembered Tate's Round Table days and how much they had meant to Georgina. He'd called her the Black Knight and thanked her for rescuing him. He was indeed a man.

Bemused by her thoughts of him, Georgina didn't hear him leave the bed until she sensed his closeness. He moved so silently that it was only as he came closer still, that she heard his quiet breathing. Had he come to switch beds again? She lowered her lashes until her eyes were mere slits, and she waited.

Quint squatted down to stare at his miracle woman, and it was then he saw—through the screen of her lashes—the glint of firelight captured in that betraying slit of her aware eyes. He smiled a little. Women were a strange race. He'd never before been tempted to try to solve one. This one was worth the effort.

What would Mrs. Adams at Field's recommend that he do under these circumstances? Pretend with Georgina that she was unaware of him? Or start talking? He was uncertain. So he solved it his way. He took action. Blanket and all, he scooped her into his arms and walked on his knees to lay her down on the warm rug between him and the warm fire.

Ready to be the one to coax and make amends, he was astonished when she freed her arms from the blanket and sneaked them around his bare shoulders. He bent his head in hopes of a kiss, so he heard her say quite clearly, "I'm sorry, Quint. I behaved abominably. I do trust you."

He'd never actually heard anyone say "abominably", so that did catch a tiny portion of his attention, but he was more surprised that he'd found a woman who could give an apology. And not a whining or coaxing one, just a firm and businesslike apology. It amazed him. It warmed the cockles of his heart. And it turned him into mush.

She lifted her mouth and his fit perfectly over hers. He gave her the sustenance of love. His kisses deepened without his permission, and he slowly rolled back to drag her on top of him, there on the hearth.

Before the smoldering fire, their flames of passion leaped and danced, licking their senses, heating the honey. She rubbed against his susceptible body as he groaned and his muscles hardened.

In the warm glow from the fireplace, they entwined. Their bodies filmed with their sexual sweat, their movements were sinuous and delicious. She stripped and climbed on top of him, but he didn't allow her way. He held her close, he let her rub her hot lure against his need until he fetched protection and gave them both surcease.

As they lay spent, Quint murmured, "I once knew a man who smiled all the time. I asked him why. He told me his woman really loved him and he was in hog heaven." Quint's arm was under Georgina and he hugged her unresisting body. He watched that happen and he smiled. "Now I believe I understand."

"You think she rolled him around on the rug?"

"That could be it." He grinned then and leaned over her to kiss her throat and along under her ear.

She murmured, "Cut it out."

"You sure lose interest fast."

"If I get any stickier, I'll wear this rug all the rest of my life."

"You think I'm just a tube of superglue?"

She couldn't prevent a weak laugh.

He kissed her nose, an eyebrow and the top of her shoulder. "I'll heat some water and wash you."

She washed herself. He watched. He found her fascinating. She blushed. That made him grin. They went to bed together and slept in each other's arms. They felt they had lived through so much together that now nothing could separate them. They had been tested, and now they would win through. George sighed with great contentment, and Quint smiled, holding her snugly against him where she belonged. For now? And he lay watchful in the night.

The next morning Georgina said logically, "We need to go to Texas before we go to Chicago."

"I've been gone too long. We need to get to Chicago. Anyway, I've met your folks."

She countered, "They met the enigmatic Quintus Finnig. I want them to meet my love."

"Am I your love?" He watched her soberly through narrowed eyes. Could such a woman really love him? Enough?

She gave him a sassy glance. "I'm... considering you. Behave and I might find some time for you. If you—" But she looked up then and saw that he was serious. She, too, sobered. "I'll still love thee when the hills have all flattened in unnumbered millions of years. My soul knows yours."

He tried to think of words to say, but he could only groan in his soul's longing and hold her tenderly. Mrs. Adams said women needed words. His mind was blank.

But she heard his groan, and she felt his hands so gentle and loving, and she lay against his bulk in contentment. Only some women need words. Some women understand. She turned her face up to his, resting her chin on his chest, and she said, "So you love me."

He saw the twinkle of teasing in her eyes and he grinned. "Yeah." So there were no problems. Not there in that lovers' hideaway. Not yet.

It was two more days before a special plow came along to clear the snowmobile trail leading to the isolated cabin. The lovers waved from their door and held up the coffeepot, but the plowman only waved back and went on.

They were free to leave.

They didn't want to go. They found excuses. The cabin had to be meticulously tidied, the woodbox filled chock-full. They worked so hard, finding another, then *another* thing to do. They cleaned the basement guns, putting them away. And they cleaned the retrieved ones to take with them. The food was sorted and some was frozen. They had nothing to pack. Their only clothes were those they stood in—he in motorcycle leather, and she in someone's coveralls. Those and the dark knit caps. They spent one more night there, reluctant to give up their paradise.

On the morning after that, they tidied after breakfast and took the car battery out and put it into the snowmobile's storage box, along with the license plates and Georgina's purse. Silently they looked around at the countryside, and at their cabin, then they looked at each other. They didn't clasp each other or kiss. They simply looked at each other. It was a silent communication that held profound meaning to them. Then Quint put on his helmet and saw to hers. They mounted the mechanical sled and slowly moved away.

When they reached the first bend, Quint stopped the machine and looked back, not at Georgina, but back toward the cabin. She was immeasurably touched by his sentiment. Sitting behind him, Georgina didn't look to the cabin but lay her helmeted head against his back and hugged him. He crossed his arms over hers on his chest and held them tightly to him before driving off along the trail, leaving the cabin behind.

At the edge of the little town they came to the shed where Quint restored the plates and put the battery back into the anonymous silvery car. He stored the snowmobile in the car's place. Then they went to Murray's service station where Quint turned over the guns from the invaders.

Murray accepted them with a grin. "You had company."

"They were just nosey," Quint replied.

"We saw the Rambo rescue." He gave George a knowing smile.

She gasped. "You were there? Why didn't you help?"

In surprise, Murray asked quickly, "Help? Who? You didn't need us, and we don't like them others."

Quint laughed and put his hand on George's nape. "Wasn't she something? She wasn't Rambo, she was the Black Knight."

"Isn't she a little pale to be a black knight?" Murray inquired.

"It's mental," Quint explained. Then he held out his hand to Murray. "I owe you. You and all the others."

"You're welcome. You done your share in past times." Then he asked, "Going out of Reno?"

Quint nodded. "Might just as well."

"We'll be watching."

"Like I said, I owe you."

"No," Murray replied. "You helped with the Irish relief all them years. We'll never be able to clear your page of the debt we owe you for it all."

The two men hugged. They became oddly emotional and a little awkward.

Murray was flushed and almost servile in telling Georgina goodbye. Being one of five Lambert sisters, she'd seen this male response before. But this time, it wasn't she who had caused that reaction. It was Murray's hero worship of Quint that had spilled over onto her. She knew how to handle it so that he didn't feel foolish.

She smiled at Murray and held out her hand. "Thanks for taking care of us. You were magnificent."

That tied Murray's tongue. He nodded and smiled and waved his hands around as the lovers left.

They hadn't even left the tiny town before Georgina began to question Quint. "What on earth did you do to cause all those people to want to go to such lengths to help you?''

"I brought along a gorgeous blonde. You had to've noticed the boss tried to get us into the chopper. He was after you. If we'd ridden with him, they would've let me see if I could fly by myself, and he'd 'a 'kept you."

"Baloney."

"Why else would he wanna give us a ride?''

She guessed, "To be sure you got out of this area, his 'territory'. Who are you and why do so many people get nervous around you, or try to help you?''

"I'm only a man."

And the problem was, he meant it. To himself, he wasn't unusual. It was only that other people reacted to him as if he was different. That was really what he thought. Now how was she going to get him to tell her what on earth he was that people reacted to him as they did? "Quint, I need to know—"

"The barrel of that gun was nasty. My head hurts. Let's let this go for a while, okay?''

But driving to Reno, he encouraged her to talk and he replied. So his banged-up head didn't demand silence; it just didn't want to talk about that one subject. As they drove into the Reno airport she inquired, "Is there anything I need to know about you for my own safety?''

And he replied, "No."

She gave him a speaking glance, and he winked at her.

Ten

————

At the airport terminal, one of the men from the intrusive helicopter smiled a greeting to Georgina and Quint. He was there to see that they got on the plane to Chicago. He offered to carry their nonexistent luggage, and he tipped his nonexistent hat to Georgina. She snubbed him. As if ordering a flunky, Quint said to him, "Watch her while I make a couple of calls."

"Glad to."

But Georgina told the flunky, "Go chase your tail."

Quint said patiently, "Georgina."

The flunky grinned as Quint went to the phone bank.

The flunky asked, "So, Georgina, you coming back home soon?"

She not only didn't acknowledge his comment, she walked off as if he wasn't there. He signaled a watchful Quint the direction, then had to hustle to catch up. "Tell me when you're gonna move," he suggested.

"You're going to roast in hell," she replied.

He loved it. "You never know."

She bought magazines and brushed past him, and she walked away as if she wore that full-length Russian lynx coat over silk, instead of camouflage coveralls and a knit cap.

She saw no reason to forgive or be kind to a man who'd tied Quint's hands and held a gun on him. She walked to the phone bank and met Quint, who was very alert and gave the flunky a flick of a glance that should have riveted his spine.

The flunky advised, "You might reconsider about this one. She's got a mind of her own. She'll be nothing but trouble. If you like, I'll take her off your hands and save you the bother."

Quint gave him a glance and replied, "You'd be mincemeat."

The flunky narrowed his eyelids in speculation, decided and sighed. "It'd be worth it."

They parted from their escort and went down the ramp for their plane. "You implied that I'd chew him up and spit him out," Georgina accused.

"No. You'd shatter him with one look."

She could accept that. "He didn't seem afraid of you. Why was that? Did he think you wouldn't attack him in this crowd? He underestimated you."

"The reason he wasn't afraid was that he knows you're the Black Knight and you stand for truth and justice. If I attacked him without a reason, he knew you'd defend him. And besides that, I'm bigger'n him, so he knows I can't pick on him.''

"I can't understand how you could be such adversaries at the cabin and almost like old friends here.''

"It's like politics. You have to get along. Maybe like dogs. You growl over a bone but you don't mind them if they keep their distance.''

"I'm not a bone.''

"A rag, a bone and a hank of hair,'' he expanded.

"What was 'the bone'? You all weren't stiff-legged over me.''

"Territory,'' he replied, saying the obvious.

She chewed on that awhile and began to understand. Then later she asked, yet again, "And you? What are you, Quintus Finnig?''

He gave her that same blank look and replied as he had before, "I'm only a man.''

"Then I'm only a woman.''

He smiled and repeated, "A woman.'' Then he put his hand possessively at her nape and held her as if he controlled her and everyone could be safe from her.

Leaving Chicago's O'Hare Airport, Quint glowered at the day. February was a terrible month in the North. This was the worst possible time of the year to introduce Georgina to his city. Piles of dirty, rotten snow lined along everywhere. Christmas was past with its decorations and fresh clean snow, spring was a long way off, and it was cold.

To help his cause, Quint took Georgina by cab to the newly renovated, elegant Marshall Field downtown on the Loop. There he introduced her to Mrs. Adams, who was courteous and never allowed one

flickering eyelash to indicate that she was quite familiar with Georgina Lambert, the lady who had caused
in Quintus Finnig the need to read poetry. Mrs. Adams
smiled and her eyes were warm and welcoming.

"How do you do?" Georgina said, and smiled
back.

Quint asked, "Did you have enough time?"

With the ease of a real professional, Mrs. Adams
replied, "You gave us such excellent directions, that
it was no trouble." She smiled at Georgina in such a
reassuring way that it puzzled the younger woman.
Then Mrs. Adams said to Quint, "The bags are here."

"I called Mrs. Adams from Reno," Quint explained. "You didn't have nothing, and I didn't think
you'd want to shop, wearing coveralls." But even as he
said that, he remembered the easy confidence Georgina displayed as she walked through Field's, and he
knew shopping in coveralls wouldn't have bothered
her. And he thought if that was really so, it answered
all his fears. But could she really adjust to his kind of
life?

Georgina frowned at the packed new suitcases.
"There was no need. My family has accounts here. I
can't allow you this inconvenience."

Mrs. Adams almost nodded as she smiled and
waited for Quintus to smooth that over, as he'd been
instructed by her.

"You can pay me back if you keep the things. Mrs.
Adams said anything that don't fit or's not right, you
can send back."

Georgina beamed at them both. "I'm so curious."

"He described you perfectly," Mrs. Adams reas-
sured her. "His description of your coloring was ex-

cellent.'' Therefore the red dress wasn't the blue-red for a brunette, but a delicious orange-red. And the shirtwaist wasn't brown but a champagne beige. Mrs. Adams was pleased that was so.

Having verified that the Lambert account was still functioning, Georgina switched the purchases to it. She then ordered a luxurious ski outfit to send to Frances to replace the lost pink one. She wrote a note for Mrs. Adams to include in the package, saying, ''Dear Frances, Anyone who could wear pink can handle purple. I gave the pink one to a man riding a motorcycle.''

Georgina read the note aloud. ''That'll drive Frances crazy.'' And she laughed.

George had wondered where Quint would lodge her, and she was terribly disappointed when she found herself deposited with her oldest sister Tate and Tate's husband, Bill, at their posh Michigan Avenue condo.

''What a lovely surprise!'' Tate said. ''Quint didn't tell us why you were flying in from Reno, just that you would be here today. I thought you were skiing.''

Georgina's relatives had greeted Quint courteously enough, but then they concentrated on her, ignoring him. ''Why are you with him?'' Bill asked Georgina.

Quint put down the two bags inside the door and stood silently, waiting for Georgina's reply.

Now, how was she supposed to tell her relatives that Quint stole her from a lodge and they stayed five days in an isolated cabin, to which a chopper had arrived carrying men with guns? She couldn't. So she said, ''We ran into each other skiing, and when he had to come back, I figured I might just as well see about expanding Bob's media-training business here in Chicago. We'd discussed it. And you know winter in Sacramento, it just rains. This seemed a good chance to come here, see you all, and get in some of the groundwork for Bob. Want to be the first to sign up, Bill?''

"I will sign up." The way he said that meant he wasn't at all satisfied with her explanation.

"You deliberately came to Chicago in February?" Bill had chosen another angle to find out why she'd shown up there.

She replied, "I prefer bone-cracking cold to rain."

"You might actually make a Chicagoan," Tate commented. "It takes peculiar people to manage."

As if directed by the word "peculiar", Bill asked Quint, "How were the slopes?"

"I don't know. We had one hell of a storm."

Bill nodded, and Quint knew then that Bill and Tate were perfectly aware of the extent of the storm. His query had been a brother-in-law's trap. So Quint asked an embarrassing question of his own. "What are you doing home today?"

Bill's eyes glinted with the word-sword question and he smiled a touché. "Family business."

Having used "taking care of personal business" as the excuse to see and take care of Georgina, Quint understood that Bill was there specifically to block Quint's intrusion into Georgina's life. Quint nodded once to acknowledge the riposte.

Bill dismissed him with, "Our thanks for delivering Tate's sister. Call, and perhaps we can arrange a time to get together. Perhaps for lunch."

But Georgina was completely aware of what Bill was doing. "I just stopped off to say hello and leave my bags. We have an errand. Could I have a key?"

She saw that Bill frowned without moving a single facial muscle. How did he do that? "Tate hasn't been feeling very well," he mentioned.

Quint instantly saw Tate's surprise over that pronouncement, and that Georgina saw it, too. "Nonsense," Tate said, "Come back when you can. I'm delighted you're here. Good luck on . . . whatever."

So Tate understood Bill, but she also understood Georgina and Quint. Bill might be opposed, but Tate was keeping hands-off. She trusted them to figure things out for themselves.

"Should I change?" George asked Quint.

"You're fine, the way you are," he replied. He had really planned to leave her with Tate, but Bill's acting so hostile got Quint's dander up.

"I'm not too clean."

Mostly to elevate Bill's blood pressure, Quint replied, "Where we're going, that won't matter." It was then that Quint decided to disillusion Georgina and let her go. It was the only way. It was only self-delusion for him to imagine that he could ever have any kind of permanent relationship with such a woman, such a lady.

So he took her through his section of Chicago. Believing that he saw as Georgina would, he was struck by the bleakness, the poverty, the needs that could never be fulfilled. He became discouraged for the first time in his life. It was hopeless. Futile. He introduced her to people and watched their eyes shift as they saw her.

But Georgina was from Texas which, in the Lamberts' time there, has seen rough years—the droughts, the wars, the booms and the depressions, and the fifty-year wet cycle that brought bugs, molds and foundered livestock. To have survived in that land, as it had been the last one hundred fifty years to have weathered all those trials, had taken people of considerable starch. So Georgina looked at the people there in Chicago and recognized their strivings. She saw the courage, the efforts, the makeshift remedies that held. She saw the love Quint had for those street people, which they returned.

"Had enough?" he asked finally, with bitterness.

She smiled at her love. "I'm hungry."

Quint looked at her with her perfectly cut, healthy hair and clean, flawless complexion, and he narrowed his eyes. "What do you know about soup kitchens?"

He was being abrasive. He expected her to be a wide-eyed novice to the realities of life. "I've helped down in Texas when I've been home," George said candidly. "I belong to a group that finds food for people where we can. We go everywhere, looking. Restaurants that fix too much, cancelled meetings where the food would be pitched, leftovers from catered parties, grocery stores that give away fruit and vegetables that are bruised or just past fresh, but can still be used in soups or salads. Bread, rolls, cakes that are past prime. All that feeds hungry people."

He grunted a sound of acknowledgement. "We do that here."

But she went on. "During Lent, we have 'hunger days' when employed people have a meal with us and give us what they ordinarily pay for lunch. This helps with rent and equipment and heating. It's all volunteer. No rake-off. And people donate paper sacks and containers for others to carry food home to their families.''

"Yeah."

"I'd be interested in seeing your operation to see if you all are doing anything that will help us. Are we going to have supper there?"

He didn't know how to back down. "Where we go, they serve only lunch. It's a hot meal, but they take home enough for supper and breakfast. We'll have a cold meal."

"I haven't a dime," she told him, having left her purse at Tate's. "Will you treat me?"

"Yeah. You're with me."

So they had cheese sandwiches with pickles and elegant hors d'oeuvres, left over from some banquet, with orange punch from another. They sat at a long table and Quint watched as Georgina spoke to those around her. They responded cautiously. When those people left, Georgina was silent.

Quint began, "You were nice to them but—"

"They seem like nice people."

"But you don't look like you belong here."

She studied him for a minute as she chewed and then she declared, "You're a snob."

"Me?" He was indignant.

"You've had everything your way all of your life."

He dismissed that. "Yeah. A street kid."

"Even that was your choice. I will bet you—lend me ten dollars—I will bet you ten dollars that you've never looked poor."

"Poor." He frowned at the word.

"Like a really poor person: defeated, hopeless. Look at these people, they have all sorts of resources—job training, clothing banks, food stamps, soup kitchens. They can come here and eat and not pay anything because they aren't asked whether or not they can pay. They have help with housing and heating. They have people like you. Their clothing is good, they move with confidence. You undoubtedly have deadbeats here—they're everywhere—but for the majority of these people, this is just temporary while they get their feet on the ground. When you were ten, there wasn't this organization yet. Who fed you?"

"Simon."

"Simon. Simon says. He must have been a wonderful man. I wish I could have known him."

"He would of said you didn't belong down here."

She leaned her chin on her hand and turned to look at him. "Are you trying to distance yourself from me? Is this your way of saying I'm not good enough for you?" She saw his pupils flare.

"We're not . . . suited," he said.

"While I am willing to concede that you are a superior man, I must say I can see no reason for you to spurn me. You don't know me well enough to make such a judgment."

"You ain't that dense."

"Why, thank you."

"Georgina, you know damned well what I mean. Quit turning my words."

She raised her chin from her hand with elaborate surprise and exclaimed, "You can't possibly think you are inferior to me. Stuff it, Finnig. I could never believe for one minute you don't recognize that you are the equal of any man. And if you are assuming anyone else can label you as the lesser, you underestimate my opinion of you." She watched him put his face in his hands and rub his forehead. He was so torn that her heart ached, but he had to see that it was only her opinion that counted.

His voice dead, he told her, "You wouldn't fit in my life. You'd be unhappy down here. This is where I live."

She knew that wasn't true. He lived on Lake Michigan, in Tate's old apartment six, just down the hall from Hillary and Angus. Quint meant that his soul was on the streets of Chicago.

"So." She was unsympathetic. "I'll be in Chicago for a while. Will you come to dinner at Tate's tomorrow? Suit and tie. Cocktails at seven."

"How do you know that?"

"Thursday-night supper for friends is a Lambert-family tradition. If there aren't any guests, it's still supper at home."

"Family friends. You want to test me?"

"There are times, Quintus Finnig, when I have doubts as to your mental workings. Were you ever dropped on your head?"

"Simon would have laughed with you. He would have loved you."

"It isn't Simon's love that I want."

Knowing the curse of curiosity infected all the Lambert daughters, Georgina wasn't at all surprised to find the newly pregnant Tate asleep on the guest-room bed, waiting up for Georgina to come back.

She smiled down on her eldest sister, and then leaned down to wiggle Tate's shoulder. "Tate," she said softly.

Tate opened her eyes without the drowsiness of most people and asked, "Are you sure about this?"

"Yes."

"Okay." Tate stood and stretched. Then she hugged Georgina briefly.

Georgina asked, "Dinner at home Thursdays?"

Tate smiled. "Yes."

"I invited Quint."

"Fine." Tate walked across to the door.

"Anyone else coming?"

With her hand on the doorknob, Tate looked back. "Probably."

"Need any help?"

Again Tate smiled and shook her head. "The house staff dotes on gatherings."

Tate told Bill at breakfast the next morning, and she wasn't at all surprised when later Bill phoned from work to add four men to the guest list. Tate sighed and warned, "She's my sister. You be very careful."

Bill replied, "That's exactly what I'm doing."

That night Georgina wore a woollen dress of a peach color that made her glow. It was one of those chosen by Mrs. Adams. The matching shoes fit perfectly.

Quint arrived at the Sawyers' elegant apartment, wearing a classic dark blue suit, white shirt and dull-red tie.

Georgina thought he looked gorgeous and smiled, the thrill of seeing him filling her lungs and licking up

the inside of her stomach. "You look nice," she said—
an understatement so that he wouldn't blush.

He gave her a small nod to acknowledge her words.

"This is one of the dresses you ordered for me," she
pointed out.

It was then that he looked at her clothing and nodded again. One of the late-arriving guests was a man
who was pleased to meet Quint. Georgina saw him
give the same kind of sign to Quint that Murray had,
and she saw Quint's solemn nod of recognition.

"So you're sure about this?" Hillary asked Georgina, indicating Quint who was standing in another
group.

"Yes." Single-word replies had become natural to
Georgina since her acquaintance with Quint.

"In for a penny, in for a pound. Sometimes I would
find it interesting to hear how you and Quint got together out yonder in California."

"You're not old enough," she told her younger sister, who groaned, having heard those words from four
older sisters all of her life.

Dinner was pleasant, the conversation erudite.
Quint was mostly silent; his comments brief and to the
point. There was one non-sister there, whose name
was Deb. She lifted her head when Quint first spoke,
then her gaze was drawn to him each time he said
something, and finally she studied him, sitting back
and watching him. He ignored her.

After they'd left the dinner table, Bill strolled over
to Georgina. "I called your boss today and told him
you were with us. He appeared a little startled to hear
that he's opening a branch of his outfit in Chicago."

"Really?" Georgina smiled at her brother-in-law. Then she talked to each man there, and to Deb, and she recruited them all. She worked on Quint, too, but he was noncommittal. Later, while other guests were leaving, Georgina lifted her mouth to Quint as he was saying good night. He did kiss her. He hesitated, but he did quickly kiss her mouth. And Deb watched that.

After the last of their guests was gone, Bill said cheerily, "That Deb's a man-eater."

"Quint's immune," Georgina replied. She hoped.

Quint called her later. "Your friends stared. They didn't know why Bill would have me there."

"They'd never seen such a potent man. And I saw Rogers give you the Murray sign."

"What's the Murray sign?"

"I'm not sure because when they moved their hands, both had their backs to me, but each made a sign with his hand. You nodded."

"I helped collect money and goods for the families of men killed in Ireland."

"And that's what started the network that you tapped in California . . . and here?"

"It's a part."

"I see," she said thoughtfully.

"Georgina, there's more. I used to run a sports gambling operation. I quit five years ago, I'm strictly legit now, but that doesn't change the fact I did it. That's why the West Coast guys were curious about me."

Again she said "I see." But this time she really understood. It all made sense.

But he didn't think she did understand. "No, you don't," he said.

"Speaking of signs, Deb's sign I recognized right away."

"She's just looking for excitement."

"What about me?"

There was the slightest pause. "That's the reason I called you, Georgina." His voice roughened. "To tell you goodbye." He cleared his throat. "I heard from the West Coast and they said they would leave you alone. It's okay for you to go home. I wish... I... I wish you all the luck in the world. God bless."

And the phone went dead.

The next morning, Georgina called her boss out in Sacramento, but before she could speak, he said, "I understand I'm opening a branch in Chicago."

"Great! I was just calling you about that very thing."

"George—"

"I've signed up seven people for the first session. When shall we begin? Shall I find a suite or a floor and shall I begin hiring?"

"If we do this now, you'll probably have to stay in Chicago," Bob warned.

"So?"

A native of California, he explained patiently, "You wouldn't be coming back to Sacramento."

"Darn," she said insincerely. Then she sighed. "Well, I suppose you will pay me a foreign service increase?"

Quite seriously, Bob agreed. "Yes." He paused. "I suspect I'd better come and find out what the hell is going on out there."

"I'll wait here."

"You do that."

Georgina hung up the phone and sought Tate who was with Benjamin. Georgina sat and watched her four-year-old nephew and just smiled. Benjamin showed her a drawing of something, which he explained. She was charmed.

"Quint is superior," Tate said. "Almost as superior as Bill."

Georgina knew better. Quint was far beyond Bill, but Tate was her sister and George loved her, so she didn't argue. "Do you still have a key to your old apartment?"

"Ah. Let me look." She left Georgina and Benjamin together while she searched, but she was unsuccessful. "Call Hillary. She may still have hers."

Hillary did.

So when Quint came into his apartment that night, just a little drunk, he found Georgina sitting on his living-room sofa, wrapped in a soft pink robe, reading a book, waiting. He was boggled. She had intended that he be. His voice didn't work and he appeared not to believe his eyes.

In despair, he whispered, "Damn you, damn you, damn you."

She smiled. "Well, hello to you, too."

He stared at her, sitting there so serenely, her blond hair haloed by the light from the reading lamp. "Are you real?"

"Of course." She got up from the sofa and went toward him.

Suffering, he watched her approach. "I gave you up."

"How foolish of you," she chided tenderly.

"My God, Georgina, don't torture me this way." But he didn't stop her from taking off his scarf and pulling his gloves from his hands.

"You're doing it to yourself," she said. "If you love me as you claim you do, there's no problem. Come, let me help you with your coat. I've made soup for you. It has a little of everything."

He was awkward and troubled. She indicated he was to sit at the table, and she served them both. He hesitated, then he realized he was hungry and began to eat.

She sat and watched him mostly, just loving the sight of this stubborn, marvelous man. No one had ever told her a man could believe that he was being noble in giving up a woman. She ought to have some say in the matter. How to convince him?

Since he no longer could impress her and he needed to convince her that he was truly unsuitable, Quint told her everything. He showed her the pictures that had sent him after her. He described how he'd contacted the network and his amazement that it still worked. Then he told her all the rest—gambling, that he'd almost been caught and it wasn't until then that he remembered Simon and how angry he'd have been with Quint.

He told her, "It's a lucrative business. There are all kinds of ways to make money at gambling, all illegal, most places. But we've been out of gambling now for over five years. Now we ship goods. We're suppliers."

"What do you ship now?"

"Nothing fancy. Used cars and auto parts to Third World countries. Clothing. Toilet paper. Discarded things, like kitchen utensils, that are still usable. People need them."

"There's money in that?"

"Not a whole lot, but it helps people—the people that glean the trash, the people that clean what's found, those that pack it, and those that transport it."

"If you pay all those people, how can you make any money at all?"

"We ship other things—small things, like medicine, mail, machine parts, cement mix—things no one else particularly wants to handle, to places no one else wants to go."

"But you go there."

"There's a satisfaction to it. You feel you help."

She smiled at him, and he began to tell her stories. Any Irishman comfortable with a listener can tell stories. He expanded and his tongue fell back to his own way of speaking. She followed him, her eyes on him softly, lovingly, and she smiled.

Gradually he became more eloquent in a reversal as he began to sell her on himself. He was honest. He was no millionaire, but he might be. He had plans. He needed backers to buy the ships. He outlined how that could be done, and she knew that he would do it all.

After a long, long time, he stopped. He leaned back in his chair and looked at his love. "How brave are you?"

"You need to ask that of a Lambert?"

"Ah, I forget you are the Black Knight. But when you are that, you're helping others. Can you help yourself?"

"I love you, Quintus Finnig."

"Do you mean the whole package, or just the loving?"

"All the way, good or bad, whatever comes."

"I would do my damnedest for you," he promised her.

"I know."

"I want you now."

She undid her hair so that it slithered down onto her shoulders. Then she stood up and unbelted her robe.

"Georgina," he said starkly, "I don't have anything to protect you."

"I do."

He shuddered, his eyes closed, and he groaned, as she gave up. He came to her and took her against him, his arms as taut and aching as his body. He squeezed her too tightly so the air whooshed from her lungs. She gave a tender, sweet, very emotional, rather teary laugh.

Then he kissed her. His kisses had always been fantastic, but this one went beyond anything she'd ever experienced. It was as if he worshiped her; as if he had a single chance for paradise, and this was it.

He stood back and looked at her, and his eyes were flames, his face pale beneath his tan. He got out of his clothes, and came to her. He parted her robe and brought her cool body to his heat. She sighed in surrender and he shivered, his breath labored.

He led her into his bedroom. She lay down on the bed and lifted her arms to him. He saw the packets on the bedside table, tore open one and put it on. Then he came to her.

Georgina supposed it was their odd adventures, the dangers they had shared and their turbulent emotions that had sensitized their flesh and feelings so that they felt each contact exquisitely. His touches were like small shocks of thrills. His kisses curled her fingers, spread her toes, lifted her chest and opened her knees.

He was rigid and single-minded. His desire took over his mind and he wooed her with purpose. She was willing. He moved her body as he tasted her and his hands caressed her marvelously. Her sounds drove him frantic and he coupled with her, and heard her groan of pleasure. Then his body made love to her—eagerly, tumultously, mind-bendingly until their passions shattered in all the amazing thrills of love.

When his breath was again under reasonable control, he said to her in a groan, "Don't ever leave me. Stay with me."

"Yes."

"Honey, are you sure you know what you're doing?"

"I'm sure."

But even after their marriage, it took a long gentle time before he believed it; before he finally realized he'd broken through the barriers he'd set against himself, and she'd met him in the middle of the street. He'd won the game. And she was his.

*   *   *   *   *

Silhouette Classics

COMING IN APRIL...

THORNE'S WAY by Joan Hohl

When *Thorne's Way* first burst upon the romance scene in 1982, readers couldn't help but fall in love with Jonas Thorne, a man of bewildering arrogance and stunning tenderness. This book quickly became one of Silhouette's most sought-after early titles.

Now, Silhouette Classics is pleased to present the reissue of *Thorne's Way*. Even if you read this book years ago, its depth of emotion and passion will stir your heart again and again.

And that's not all!

Silhouette Special Edition

COMING IN JULY...

THORNE'S WIFE by Joan Hohl

We're pleased to announce a truly unique event at Silhouette. Jonas Thorne is back, in *Thorne's Wife*, a sequel that will sweep you off your feet! Jonas and Valerie's story continues as life—and love—reach heights never before dreamed of.

Experience both these timeless classics—one from Silhouette Classics and one from Silhouette Special Edition—as master storyteller Joan Hohl weaves two passionate, dramatic tales of everlasting love!

CL-36

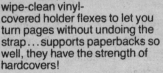
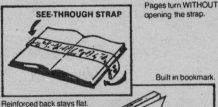

NAVY BLUES
Debbie Macomber

Between the devil and the deep blue sea...

At Christmastime, Lieutenant Commander Steve Kyle finds his heart anchored by the past, so he vows to give his ex-wife wide berth. But Carol Kyle is quaffing milk and knitting tiny pastel blankets with a vengeance. She's determined to have a baby, and only one man will do as father-to-be—the only man she's ever loved...her own bullheaded ex-husband!

You met Steve and Carol in NAVY WIFE (Special Edition #494)—you'll cheer for them in NAVY BLUES (Special Edition #518). (And as a bonus for NAVY WIFE fans, newlyweds Rush and Lindy Callaghan reveal a surprise of their own....)

Each book stands alone—together they're Debbie Macomber's most delightful duo to date! Don't miss

**NAVY BLUES
Available in April,
only in *Silhouette Special Edition*.
Having the ''blues'' was never
so much fun!**